Mad Dog

Tyndale House Publishers, Inc. • Carol Stream, Illinois

STARLIGHT

2

Animal Rescue

Mad Dog

DANDI DALEY MACKALL

Visit Tyndale's website for kids at www.tyndale.com/kids.

You can contact Dandi Daley Mackall through her website at
www.dandibooks.com.

TYNDALE and Tyndale's quill logo are registered trademarks of
Tyndale House Publishers, Inc.

Mad Dog

Designed by Jacqueline L. Nuñez

Edited by Stephanie Voiland

Scripture quotations are taken from the *Holy Bible*, New Living
Translation, copyright © 1996, 2004, 2007 by Tyndale House
Foundation. Used by permission of Tyndale House Publishers, Inc.,
Carol Stream, Illinois 60188. All rights reserved.

For manufacturing information regarding this product, please call
1-800-323-9400.

ISBN 978-1-4143-1269-9

Printed in the United States of America

15   14   13
 8   7   6   5

Get rid of all bitterness, rage, anger, harsh words, and slander. . . . Instead, be kind to each other, tenderhearted, forgiving one another, just as God through Christ has forgiven you. Ephesians 4:31-32

IF THE WORLD had any idea how mad I, Wesley "Mad Dog" Williams, am at it, the sun would be too scared to show its ugly face around here.

I squint up at the giant burning ball of fire that's making me sweat through my T-shirt. Nothing to do but hustle up the frying-hot sidewalk and take the steps two at a time. I have to pass under the big sign I've walked under dozens of times. It still gets to me. Black letters over the door read, "Nice Animal Shelter."

Right.

This place is no shelter. And there's not an animal in there feeling nice.

The problem is, the whole town is named "Nice." A great place to live if you like ice-cream socials and community picnics.

I don't. But I'm not living in Nice forever. Not even close.

As soon as my mom gets out of rehab, I'm moving back to Chicago, getting a job in the city, and finding an apartment with a little backyard for Rex, my dog. And I'm going to train a dog for Mom so she can have one of man's best friends all to herself.

Nice, Illinois, is about the last place any-body from my old crew in Chicago would expect to find me. That's for sure. Nobody in Nice calls me Mad Dog. But Mad Dog is still how I think of myself. The handle fits, even in Nice. Maybe *especially* in Nice.

I glance up again at the Nice Animal Shelter sign. Some joke. I've seen my fair share of ugly in my 14 years on this planet, but I've never seen nothing uglier than a dog pound. And that's what this is, no matter how you call it. It's a dog pound. Pounds are like death row for the innocent, without trials.

I take a deep breath, yank the door open, and walk in. A blast of cold air hits me. You can bet the "Nice" animals don't have air-conditioning in back. Even out here in the lobby, with crisp, cool air blowing through like March winds, it smells like rotten cat food and ammonia.

"May I help you?" asks a blonde I've never seen before. Her skin is so white I can't believe she's ever seen the sun. Not this month anyway. Not August in Illinois. I've seen snow less white than this girl.

I figure she must be new, maybe a temp. Everybody who is anybody gets out of town in August.

My mom used to talk about taking a vacation to Florida. That was back when I was young enough to think Disney World was cool and the Mouse was real.

"Dog warden in?" I ask, walking up to the big desk in the center of the lobby.

"He's out all week on vacation," she answers. "Would you like to fill out an application to adopt a pet?" She holds up a one-page application I've filled out a couple dozen times before.

"I'm on file." I hear my own voice like it's someone else's. The words come out sharp as blades and cold as hailstones. I tell myself that I've got nothing against this girl. I'm just angry at the people who let their animals end up in a place like this.

The girl looks worried, though. I'm not big, but I *am* black. A definite minority in Nice. *She'd* be the minority in my old neighborhood, the projects on the south side of Chicago.

Anyway, I know there's no hint of friendly on my face. So chances are I'd be making this big-smile cheerleader nervous, no matter what color I was.

"Why don't you have a seat over there and fill out the application?" The girl holds out the paper again. "It should only take you a few minutes." Her smile is back. "We have a full load of pets to choose from today."

Somehow, knowing that death row is full doesn't make me feel like smiling.

Before I can tell her this, the skinny woman who runs the pound on Thursdays comes in through the silver double doors behind the desk.

With her come the cries and barks of strays caged and waiting for their fate. Tomorrow, Friday, is execution day at the pound. They call it "putting them to sleep" or "euthanasia" or "putting them down" or just "taking care of it."

The skinny woman is wearing a gray uniform that makes her look like a mail carrier. Her name's Wanda, unless she always wears somebody else's uniform. *Wanda* is written in yellow letters on her front pocket.

"It's you again, huh?" She says this without smiling, and I like that. At least she's not a fake.

Wanda turns to the receptionist. "Wes is okay. You can always let him come through. We keep applications on file for him. He works with the Coolidges on their farm. You know. That animal rescue outside of town. Starlight Animal Rescue."

"You work *there*?" the blonde girl says.

"Yeah." She seems so blown away by this news that I'm tempted to tell her I don't just work there. I live there. But she probably couldn't handle that.

"Do you know Hank Coolidge?" She's wide-eyed and just short of panting.

Hank is my 16-year-old . . . what? Foster brother, I guess. He's the only real son of the

5

people I live with, the Coolidges. Right now there are four of us—three fosters and Hank.

Every girl in Nice seems to have a crush on Hank. I don't get it, but there it is.

"I know him," I admit finally.

"Will you tell him Lissa says hi?" she asks. She makes me think of a collie puppy I found a home for a few months ago. Way too eager, but most people go for that.

Instead of giving her the promise that I'll be her messenger boy, I turn back to Wanda.

Wanda gets it, I think. She heads back to the silver doors and nods for me to follow.

The dogs hear us coming and start yapping and barking. Canine SOS calls drown out all other sounds except the banging of wire cages.

"So how's it going, Wes?" Wanda shouts over the howls.

This Wanda character is okay. But I'm not about to let her all up in my business. Or anybody else neither. A "how's it going?" from anybody always gets an "I'm all right" from me.

Still, for a second, I think about answering that question for real: *How am I? Well, my mom's still in rehab. I haven't seen her since February, haven't talked to her in three months, two weeks, four days—but who's counting? I don't know if I can wait nine more days to see her in person. That's when she'll walk out of that rehab place. I had to leave the only home I ever knew in Chicago, and now I'm in foster care, living on a farm with a local teen idol named Hank and two foster girls, one with cancer and the other with attitude. The only place I hang out is this pound, where they kill most of the animals I can't take with me. So how am I? You figure it out.*

"I'm all right," I answer.

The stench of the pound back here is so strong I can feel it on my skin. It makes me want to take a long, hot shower.

"What's up with this one?" I ask, pointing to a medium-size, white, short-haired mutt with a rat's tail. She's curled in the far corner of her filthy cage.

Wanda's a head taller than me. I have to stand on tiptoes so I can see the dogs in the top row of metal cages. The dog I'm pointing to hasn't moved since we got back here. But her eyes are sharp. She hasn't missed a move I've made since I walked into this pit.

7

"That quiet one? Not sure," Wanda answers. "We thought she was sick when she came in. I kept her quarantined for 48 hours. But there's nothing physically wrong with her. She got scooped up in a canvass across the tracks, up north."

"Terrier mix?" I guess. I'm also guessing the dog's smart and maybe four years old.

Wanda sighs, and it makes me think she really does care about the dogs they catch. Maybe. "I was hoping the owner would come for this one," she says. "She's so pathetic. I showed her to four people looking for a pet, but they wanted playful."

"Did they wind up with puppies?" I ask. It's what most people want. Everybody thinks they can do a better job raising things than somebody else did. They don't even think about what's best for the dogs. They only think about themselves.

"Exactly," Wanda answers.

I move down the row of cages because I have to. I have to keep moving. If I don't, I think I might kick something. Anything. It just makes me crazy that people do this to animals. To dogs that never hurt anybody.

I wish I could take all of them with me. Set every dog free, like in one of those cartoon movies.

But I learned a long time ago—life is no funny cartoon movie.

TWO

SINCE I CAN'T FREE EVERY DOG at this pound, all I can do is rescue as many dogs as I can. I have to pick the ones I know I can train and then adopt out. Hank does the same thing with horses, and now Dakota, the newest foster, helps him.

Kat, the youngest foster, tames cats. One time she pulled a sack full of kittens from the pond because she heard them crying. Nobody else heard them. Just Kat. Somebody must have dropped those scrawny kittens into the water to drown them right before Kat walked by. She nursed every last kitten back to health and found homes for them too. That's what goes on at Starlight Animal Rescue. I admit that if you've got to be in foster care, the Rescue is about as good as it gets.

Anyway, I need likable family dogs people will want in their homes, with their kids. It's not that hard to figure out some of these strays would never make it in anybody's home.

One ratty, dirt-brown dog that's as big as me lunges at the cage when Wanda strolls by. I shuffle closer for a better look, and the dog glares at me with beady brown eyes. Then she breaks into barking, showing off long, sharp teeth made for biting.

A couple of the other dogs bare teeth to the gums when I get too close to their cages.

One dog looks friendly enough. Her tail wags every time I walk by. But she's ugly as sin, like a boxer or bulldog that got left in the dryer too long. I know from experience she'd be hard to place with a mug like that.

In the corner cage on the bottom row, a black and tan short-haired mix with long, floppy ears is playing with a scrap of paper, the only "toy" in his cage. It reminds me of when I lived with my mom in a room above the bar. My favorite toys were bottle caps she'd bring home from beers she and her friends had drained. I used to make forts and trucks out of those things.

"Beagle-Lab mix, maybe?" I guess. The dog's skeleton-skinny, so it's hard to tell the age, but I'd guess about six months old.

Wanda shrugs. "The warden said the dog's owner claimed he had no idea how the four dogs and six cats we found starving in his basement got there."

"Did they arrest the guy?" This junk goes on all the time, and people go right on like nothing ever happened. Like, *Big deal—they're only animals, right?*

Wanda raises her eyebrows. "Arrest him? I doubt it."

"Right." My mind fills with pictures of what I'd like to do to that guy if I ever run into him—and those pictures are rated R for violence. It makes my head buzz, and I feel a major headache coming on. I whip off my ball cap and wipe sweat from my forehead. There's definitely no air-conditioning back here.

A long-haired runt that could be a full-blooded Pomeranian pants in one of the center cages. His tongue is as long as his pointy ears. He risks a few sideways glances at me. No stare-downs from this little guy. His tail hasn't stopped wagging since we got here. He's alert, ears pricked and pointed straight at me. His lop-sided grin invites me to come closer. Everything about this dog says he's friendly.

"How long has *he* been here?" I can't figure out why nobody's taken this dog home.

"Came in last Tuesday," Wanda answers.

"How come nobody grabbed him up?"

But right then the Pom struggles to stand, and I have my answer. He's three-legged. The fourth leg, the back left, hasn't even been cut off clean. Part of it dangles at his side like a gnarled hot dog.

"Two families thought hard about adopting the Pom, but the hanging leg was a turnoff," Wanda explains.

I feel sick to my stomach, the way I do, sooner or later, every time I come to the pound. I tell myself what I always tell myself: *Life's tough, Mad Dog. Don't let it get inside you.*

Pacing the rows of cages one more time, I pass the beagle-Lab mix. He rolls over on his side, then keeps rolling onto his back, legs curled in the air, ribs sticking out.

And he's got me. "I'll take the Blab."

"The what?" Wanda asks.

"Beagle-Lab. Blab."

"Gotcha." She grabs the ring of keys hooked to her belt.

I've taken so many dogs off her hands that we've cut the paperwork down. Anyway, the pound's application is nothing compared to the one I make people fill out before I'll let them adopt from Starlight Animal Rescue.

"Just the one this time?" Wanda asks.

"Nope." I pull three leashes out of the pockets of my baggy jeans.

"Three?" Wanda asks. She knows two's my limit. Hard enough to train two dogs at once.

But this time I'm getting the dogs for something special. "You know old Mrs. Coolidge?"

"Everybody knows Georgette Coolidge," Wanda says.

It's the truth. The woman is a real character. Her son Chester Coolidge is my foster dad. Also a character. Mrs. Coolidge doesn't even like animals that much. But she keeps finding abused animals and sending them to the Rescue.

She sends us people too—prospective pet owners. The old woman makes me a little crazy, but she's a good one to have on our side.

"So what's that lady up to now?" Wanda asks. She unlocks the Blab's cage, and he jumps out. But he doesn't run off. Wanda snaps on the leash and hands me the dog.

I reach down and scratch the dog's back and chest, then behind his floppy ears. First thing I'll do is fatten him up. "Mrs. Coolidge has been pressuring the nursing home, Nice Manor, to pilot a pet program with some of their assisted-living people," I explain. "Don't know that much about it, but I'm getting dogs ready in case it works out."

"If that woman is pushing for it, I have no doubt the program will go through," Wanda says. "So, you give dogs to the nursing home residents?"

"Not exactly." I never just *give* dogs to anybody. Not even to Mrs. Coolidge. "I'll pretrain the dogs first. Then I'll pretrain the old people. After that, I'm not sure. Guess we'll see how it plays out. Mrs. Coolidge seems to think it's going to work."

The Blab tosses his head and jerks the

leash, making me think he's never had a leash before.

Wanda untangles the Blab's leash for me. "Where do you start?"

"I want the dogs to bond with the old people. Not just with me. So I'll get them to help with the basic obedience training. That way the dogs can bond with *them*."

"Bet the old folks will like that," Wanda says. "My great-aunt's in one of those nursing homes up in Cleveland. She should get a dog. Might give her something to talk about besides her aches and pains."

"If everything works out and the dogs bond with the old people, then Mrs. Coolidge says I can do more advanced training."

Wanda scrunches up her face. She's bone-skinny but still has two chins when she makes this face. "Don't tell me Mrs. Coolidge plans on getting those old folks to show the dogs at dog shows." She eyes the Blab, who has been chewing on my shoelaces for the last few minutes.

"Nah. Not that kind of advanced training. Practical stuff. Like if somebody's deaf, we can train her dog to nudge her when the phone rings or when somebody knocks at the door.

17

I could train the dogs to fetch things for people when they're in bed or in a wheelchair. Stuff like that."

"That's pretty cool, Wes," Wanda says. "So, made up your mind on the other two dogs yet?"

We both stare at the cages. This is the hardest part. It's like choosing which dogs will live and which won't. I hate this part.

"Better give me two females," I tell her. We both know female dogs are easier to housebreak.

She nods, then glances at her watch. "What about that Chihuahua you got here a while back? Wouldn't that one make a good nursing home dog?"

"I placed Taco last month." I miss that dog, but the guy who took Taco was a perfect match. Retired, fussy, and a guy who kept his house warm enough for Taco.

The terrier is still cowering in the back of her cage. "Let me see the terrier mix."

Wanda opens the cage, but she has to lift the dog out. She hands the trembling dog to me. As soon as I have her, the terrier buries her nose in the crook of my elbow. She's scared, but she's not scared of me. Probably the noise around here.

I shouldn't take her. She's too shy. She won't like the noise of a group home. Plus, she's old enough to have bad habits.

The dog pokes her snout deeper into the crook of my elbow.

I know better than to fall for "cute." This dog is all wrong for a noisy nursing home, where dozens of people could grab for her at the same time.

I scratch her back, and her tail wags. "I'll take her," I say, regretting it as soon as the words are out.

"Thought you would," Wanda says.

"And that ugly female over there." It's not the bulldog's fault she's so ugly.

"This one?" Wanda asks, going right to the dog. No doubt which one I mean. "I'm guessing this dog's going to a blind person, right?" She laughs and opens the cage.

"Not a bad idea," I admit.

Wanda helps me leash the three dogs. It's a good start. It won't be easy training three at the same time. But they're good-natured.

Doors swoosh open, and footsteps sound

19

up the hall. The blonde receptionist appears. She rushes toward us but stops before she reaches the cages.

"Hank's here!" she cries, like she's announcing an early Christmas. "He's right outside! Honking for you."

"Okay." I turn to go, but I hear dog toenails scratching on a cage floor. I shouldn't glance back at the dogs I'm leaving, but I can't help it.

It's the Pomeranian making all the fuss. With his three legs, he scrambles to his feet and barks. Just once. But it feels like he's talking to me. I'd almost forgotten about my headache. Now it creeps back, pounding with every yap of the Pomeranian.

The bulldog and the beagle-Lab are pulling at their leashes, stretching me in opposite directions. The poor terrier tries to lie down between my shoes.

And the Pomeranian keeps barking.

"Hank's waiting!" the receptionist shouts, like she's afraid he'll get away.

I've already got more work than I can handle at Starlight Animal Rescue. Plus, I've got my own dog, Rex, to walk. Not to mention the fact that I need to train a dog for my mom.

"Yeah. I'm coming." I shuffle as far as the silver doors. Then I hear the Pom's single bark again.

I stop. The terrier crawls between my shoes. The Blab gets the leash in his teeth. The ugly-as-sin dog is tangled in the terrier's leash.

But I can't leave that three-legged dog.

I sigh, big and heavy. I don't need this. Three dogs are already too many. A three-legged, scrawny, good-for-nothing dog wouldn't be a lick of good in a nursing home.

Wanda passes me and shoves open the silver door. I hear Hank's horn honking outside.

"Wait!" I shout. "I'm taking the tripod."

THREE

"You've got to be kidding me!" Hank yells out the truck window.

I'm carrying the gimpy Pom and dragging the scared, rat-tailed terrier, while the beagle-Lab and ugly-as-sin bulldog tangle each other with their leashes. They trip over themselves racing for the burned grass to do their business.

"I've been frying in the truck waiting for you," Hank hollers. He scoots out, slamming his door behind him. "Four? How did you end up with four dogs, Wes?"

I hate it when Hank gets on his big-brother

act. So I don't answer. He's not the boss, no matter what he thinks.

He strides up to me, his long legs covering the distance in a few steps. "How are you going to handle all these dogs?"

It's the question I've been asking myself. My head pounds harder every time I think about how much work I'm getting myself into. I can't do this by myself. Somebody's going to have to help me. And I don't like asking anybody for help.

The terrier jumps up on Hank. It's the first brave move the dog's made, and it takes both of us by surprise.

Hank squats down and pets the terrier. "Hey, little guy."

"Girl," I say, correcting Hank. I hand over the terrier's leash, knowing Hank will take it.

Truth is, Hank can bark, but he never bites. The guy wouldn't last two days in the projects. He and I argue all the time, but Hank's usually the one to give in. He can't seem to stay mad at me longer than a few minutes. Man, are we different. And Hank doesn't hold grudges, not as far as I can tell anyway. If he did, he'd have a truck full of grudges against me.

The terrier keeps jumping on Hank, like she's not a bit scared. Hank picks her up. "I don't get it, Wes. You've never come home with this many dogs before. What were you thinking?"

"You know, Hank," I begin, "you're right, as usual. Four dogs are just too many, man. Why don't you go take that terrier back to the pound? Only you better hurry. They're killing the leftover strays tomorrow."

Hank narrows his eyes at me. We both know he won't go there. He strokes the terrier's back, and she nestles her nose right under Hank's arm. It's a good trick, and it works.

"Let's get out of here," Hank says.

Hank doesn't help me with the other dogs, so I have to wrestle the bulldog and the Blab into the only two kennels I brought along, while I keep the Pomeranian tucked under one arm. If this is any kind of preview of how things are going to go, I'm in big trouble. I have to get somebody to help me train these dogs.

We don't talk until we're out of Nice and onto the gravel road. The Blab hasn't stopped barking since the engine started. The bulldog is slobbering all over the kennel. Some of it dribbles through to the truck seat. I block the view so Hank can't see.

"I guess Gram Coolidge really worked a number on you, huh?" Hank says. "When does she want the dogs ready for the Manor residents?"

"Next Friday. But I'm going to talk her into giving me more time." The Pom tries to stand, and I have to catch him before he wiggles off the seat.

"Can you even train dogs that fast?" Hank asks.

"Depends," I answer. "Won't be easy. All by myself." This is as close as I can get to asking for help without coming out and asking. Like I said, I hate asking anybody for anything. Part of me wants to pray Hank will get the hint and volunteer to help me out. But I guess I'm not big on asking God for things either.

"You think the dogs are housebroken already?" Hank asks, not getting my hint.

"Maybe," I answer. "That little terrier on your lap—she's probably trained."

"You think?" Hank asks, like he's a proud parent. He keeps one hand on the wheel and one on the dog.

"Still," I try again, "it's going to be tough to find time to walk all four of these new dogs, plus Rex. I'll have to fatten a couple of them up. They've all got to learn some manners before I take them to Nice Manor. And don't forget, soon as I move back to Chicago, you guys are going to have to take over anyway. It would be good if somebody besides me knew how to train dogs."

Hank doesn't take the bait. He can't be that thick.

We're to the dirt road a mile from the farm. I'm never going to have a better chance than right now to get Hank to help me. "Hank?" I clear my throat.

He glances at me, then back to the road. "Yeah?"

My head's buzzing again. Hank isn't making this easy. He probably knows exactly what I want, but he's going to make me beg for it. "So, can you help?"

"With the dogs?" Hank asks, like he didn't know what I was getting at.

"No, Hank. With the elephants. Yeah! The dogs. I need help, man. It's too much for me to pull off by myself."

"You should have thought of that before, Wes," Hank says, all big-brotherish. "I don't have enough time to work the horses the way I should. I need to get the two new ones under saddle before school starts. I'm trying to help Dakota with Blackfire. I just don't have time to work with the dogs, too."

Hank turns the truck up the drive. He hits a bump, and the kennels rattle.

"Watch where you're going, will you?" I snap.

"I'm sorry, Wes," Hank says. "About not being able to help with the—"

"Forget it." But *I* won't. Just wait until he needs me to do something for him.

I stare out the window as the barn and farmhouse come into view. Annie's minivan isn't there. Annie Coolidge is my foster mom, and she's probably still at the hospital. She's a surgeon in a cancer hospital, although you'd never guess it looking at her.

Before Hank can pull the truck around the barn to park, I tell him to stop. "Just give me a minute to unload the dogs. You can spare a minute, can't you, Hank? If you'd be so kind? I don't want to put you out or anything." I've got sarcasm down cold. It's the one thing I can do better than Hank.

Hank stops the truck, but he doesn't make one move to help me unload the dogs.

Fine. I put the Pom on the seat of the truck and back out of the cab. Keeping one eye on the tripod dog, I unload the two kennels, with the Blab and the bulldog inside. When I reach across the seat for the terrier, the dog buries its nose under Hank's arm.

"I can get him," Hank says. "*Her*," he corrects, before I can.

"Don't bother." I grab for the terrier. My arm brushes the Pomeranian, and he slides off the seat.

"Look what you made me do!" I shout.

"Is he okay?" Hank asks, reaching for the Pom.

I shove his hand away. "What do you care?"

"Don't be like that, Wes."

I pick up the Pom in one hand. With the other hand, I scoop the terrier out of Hank's arms. Then I stumble out of the truck, a dog under each arm, the kennels at my feet. The Blab is barking nonstop. I kick the truck door shut. Hard.

Behind me, more barking starts. This is familiar barking.

"Rex!" I call. "Stop it."

He doesn't stop it. Rex is my German shepherd. I rescued him the second week I came to this farm. Somebody had dumped the dog on the side of the road and left him for dead. I nursed him back to health. In a way, I guess Rex rescued me, too. Until he showed up, I missed my mom and Chicago so much that I hated everything else. It felt disloyal to like the Coolidges.

Rex changed that. He taught me about dogs too. I'd always liked dogs, but I didn't know they liked me until Rex came along. When I leave this place, Rex is coming with me.

I want to pet my dog, but my arms are full. "Easy, Rex," I tell him. "I just brought you some buddies. That's all."

My foster dad comes jogging out of the house, waving. His real name is Chester, but I call him "Popeye." If you saw him, you'd know why—short, stocky, bald. He's a volunteer fireman, a farmer, and a stay-at-home dad.

I don't know what he's going to say about me bringing back four dogs. He's smiling, but he's always smiling. He shouts something to me, but I can't make it out because of Rex.

"Can't hear you!" I shout. "Rex won't quit barking at the new dogs."

Popeye walks up and takes the Pom from my arms. "Rex isn't barking at the new dogs, Wes. Don't kid yourself. That dog is barking at *you*. What are you so mad about this time?"

I frown at Popeye. The Pom is already trying to lick Popeye's sunburned head.

Rex is still barking. Popeye's right. My dog is barking at me. He knows me better than any human ever has, better than I know myself. Popeye calls him my anger-meter, my mad alarm. Rex only barks when I'm angry. And he doesn't stop until I cool off.

I give up trying to make Rex stop barking. The way I feel right now, my dog is going to be barking forever.

FOUR

POPEYE HELPS ME CARRY the kennels to the screened-in porch. He and Hank added it on a couple of years ago, before I got here. The porch runs the length of the house, so it's a great place for the foster dogs to sleep.

"This is a cute little guy," Popeye says when he sets down the bulldog's kennel, "if he didn't slobber so much." He wipes his hands on his jeans.

"Female," I correct. "I just hope you're not the only person in the world who thinks this dog is cute." In broad daylight, the dog's wrinkles have multiplied.

When I set down the terrier, she clings to the porch's wood floor like she's afraid she might fall off.

Popeye is still staring at the bulldog. "Female? Are you certain, Wes?" He shakes his head. "Wonder what my Annie will think about this one. Wonder what *Mother* will think of this one."

I hadn't thought about that. But Mrs. Coolidge left it up to me to pick the dogs. Too bad if she doesn't like my picks.

The Blab looks more restless than usual, and the Pom is whimpering. I know I should walk all the dogs, but I need help. "Popeye, would you mind–?"

Before I can ask, he blurts out, "Yikes! I better get going. We have a meeting at the fire-house. Looks like I'll be late again."

He yanks his fireman's jacket off the coat-rack, even though it's a thousand degrees out-side. "Wes, if my Annie gets home before I do, tell her I miss her and can't wait to see her. I'll make dinner when I get home."

I nod. He and Annie have been married forever. But when they're apart for, like, an hour, Popeye can't stand it. Then when they're together again, they both act like they're long-lost lovers.

"Wes?" Kat calls from the top of the stairs.

Popeye stops at the door. "Everything okay, Kat?"

"Fine," she answers. "Aren't you late for your firehouse meeting?"

I catch Popeye glancing at the kitchen clock. But he turns a smile up toward Kat. "I'm okay. You sure *you're* okay?"

"Yeah. Only what's with all the barking?" She takes the steps one at a time. Bright red hair springs all around her face, making her a pretty good double for Orphan Annie, minus the freckles. The hair's not hers because she lost all of hers when she had the second round of chemo treatments.

Two cats trail behind her. They're never far from Kat, although they won't let the rest of us near them. Fine with me.

"Hey, Kat," I call.

"Hey, Wes," she says back.

When they dropped me off at Starlight Animal Rescue and I met Kat for the first time, I got her all wrong. Number one, I thought she was way younger than she is. She's 11 now, but she could pass for eight or nine . . . until you talk to her. Two, I thought she was a "bio" Coolidge, like Hank, because she calls Annie and Popeye "Mom" and "Dad." And three, I thought she was posing, faking it, because she seemed almost too good to be true. Wrong again. There's nothing fake about her.

"Wish I could have gone to the animal shelter with you," Kat complains. She's taking the stairs extra slow. Not a good sign.

"Yeah, right. And make me haul off a dozen more cats to find homes for?" I tease.

She reaches the landing and stares at the pound dogs. "Wes! Four? You brought home four dogs?" Unlike Hank, Kat sounds totally cool with this fact. "They're adorable!" she exclaims. She goes straight for the three-legged Pomeranian, leans down, and lets him lick her face.

"Wes has his hands full this time," Popeye says. He glances at the kitchen clock again. "Gary is going to set *me* on fire if I'm any later to the fire station. I've got to go, Kat. Will you be okay until my Annie gets home? Wes is here. Dakota and Hank are out in the barn."

"Go." Kat stands up too fast. She reaches

for the doorknob to steady herself. I take a step for her, but she waves me away.

Popeye's back is to her, so I don't think he saw how dizzy she got.

"You better hurry, Dad." She opens the door she's leaning on. "Wes and I will walk the dogs. Right, Wes?"

I grin at her. She's helped me with the dogs before.

Popeye shakes his head. "No strenuous exercise until my Annie gives you the A-OK."

Annie isn't just Kat's foster mother. She's Kat's doctor. That's how Kat ended up at Starlight. She was a cancer patient in the hospital where Dr. Annie works. Nobody, not even Kat, talks about Kat's real mom and dad. But one day Dr. Annie brought Kat home with her, and I guess that was that. Hank says Kat's been on the farm ever since. Popeye and Annie are adopting Kat for real. It's almost final.

Popeye asks me to help him carry some things to the truck, but I know he just wants to talk to me without Kat around. When we're outside, he says, "Wes, don't let her walk those dogs, okay? Her immunities are still down, and so's her energy. I don't want her overdoing it."

I nod. I could have used the help, but I wouldn't do anything to hurt Kat.

When Popeye's gone, I head back inside. My brain's spinning, trying to figure out how I'm going to walk five dogs by myself.

"Let me help, Wes," Kat begs, her blue eyes getting so wide they sink even deeper into her head. "It won't hurt me to walk a dog. I can walk really slow." She tries to prove it by doing a Frankenstein shuffle toward the Pom.

I have to think fast. "Great." I pick up the Pomeranian. "Only you know what, Kat? What I really need is somebody to hold this little guy while I walk the other dogs. Would you do that? Maybe hold the Pom while you sit on the couch and watch TV or something?"

"Really?" Kat says. "I'd love that!" She glides over to the terrier and pets her. "What about this one, Wes? She looks so scared." The little dog is still hugging the floor, head low and ears drooped. "You poor little scaredy-cat dog," Kat coos. "How'd you like to sit on my lap too?" She reaches down to pick up the terrier and gets the dog up as far as her knees. Then she has to set it down again.

I'm not sure what's wrong, but I've learned

not to draw attention to whatever it is. Kat's trying hard to live a normal life. I figure the least I can do is go along with it. Still, not helping Kat is the hardest part about living here.

"Kat, could you hold off on the terrier?" I snap the dog's leash back on her. "Let me take her for a walk first."

By the time I get back to the house with the terrier, Kat's gone back to bed and the Pomeranian is asleep on the couch. Kat's left me a note:

Wes, I had to go to bed. Sorry. The Pomeranian fell asleep, so I think he'll be okay until you get back. Sorry again.
Love,
Kat

I tiptoe up the stairs and stand outside her room for a few minutes. I don't hear her snoring, but I don't hear her throwing up either.

It takes me over two hours to walk four dogs. I have to walk them one at a time. Each dog has a different problem with the routine. All the bulldog wants to do is eat flowers, roll in the grass, and jump on me—a habit I better break fast, before introducing her to old people. The terrier gets frightened by every crack of a twig and rustle of grass. When a crow caws, the poor dog goes to pieces.

The Pom takes so long to do his business that I almost give up. But I don't. The beagle-Lab, the Blab, chases everything, from flies to imaginary cars.

Poor Rex tags along until he gets bored. He's got to be wondering why I'm not running him across the field like I always do. But he doesn't bark or complain.

When I'm done walking all four dogs, plus Rex, I settle the Blab and the bulldog out on the front porch. It's closed in, so as long as people are careful going in and out, there shouldn't be a problem.

The terrier and the Pomeranian are too needy to leave on the porch. I can let them stay with Rex and me in my bedroom until they get used to the farm. With one dog under each arm, I head upstairs to my room.

It still feels funny to think of it as *my room*. This is the first space I've had that's mine and nobody else's. I've lived by myself, but it's not the same thing. Once, when I was 12, I lived alone for a week. My mom hooked up with a really bad dude, a guy I called "T," for Troll, although he and Mom thought I called him T 'cause his name was Tyrone. He stole her paycheck once and went off and got high on it. When Mom disappeared with the troll, I didn't tell anybody. Finally a social worker came to the house and told me my mother was okay and would be in jail for a couple of weeks. I had to stay in a home for boys until she got out. I'm never going back there.

I open the door to my room. Even though I've been here a year, I don't have anything on the white walls except a calendar. And I only have that so I can cross out the days until I see Mom again. Hank and Annie keep trying to give me posters and stuff to put up. But I don't want to put anything up. I'm not staying. Not like Kat. I'm just passing through. I keep the walls bare so we all remember that.

Wooden beams stretch across the rough, white ceiling and crisscross down two of the walls. It makes me feel like I'm in a castle or one of those old inns you see in movies. You can almost picture knights and dragons lurking outside. That's something I'd never say out loud though, even if they tortured me in the castle dungeon. I've got two windows, a dresser, a desk, a bed, and a huge chest, where I keep my dog aids—things like rubber balls, treats, ropes, and leashes.

"Here you go, little Pom," I say, putting the dog in the middle of an old blanket and folding it into a nest.

I fish a dog bed out from under my bed and place the terrier in it. "There you go, scaredy-cat dog." It's hard not to go ahead and name the dogs. But I want the old folks at Nice Manor to name their own dogs. Naming is one of the most important things a dog owner does.

I sit on the floor for a while, petting and scratching the dogs until I can sneak away from them. Rex is waiting for me outside my door.

"You're all that, dog. Know what I'm saying?" I stroke his big head until his ears flop back and his tongue hangs out.

Rex leads me on a long walk through the pasture. At the far end of the property, I see Hank riding Starlight, his horse. I know it's Starlight because I can see the brown and white spots. If I didn't know the Paint was blind, I'd never be able to tell it by the way Hank's galloping her now.

The mare was born blind and her owner was going to put her down, but Hank talked him out of it. Still makes me mad when I imagine somebody doing that just because the horse got off to a bad start being blind and all. Hank named her Starlight, and that was the beginning of Starlight Animal Rescue.

I don't ride, but supposedly Hank's the best at it. Of course. Like with everything else.

"Wes!" Hank shouts. Out of the corner of my eye, I see him wave.

But I'm still mad at Hank for refusing to help me with the dogs. So I act like I don't hear him or see him. Hank is pretty easy to fool.

Rex and I turn around, and my dog starts barking. I tell him to stop, but he keeps it up. I might have fooled Hank, but I never fool Rex.

WHEN REX AND I GET BACK, there's a black truck parked by the barn. I recognize the truck from Tri-County Animal Clinic. The Nice vets get called out here all the time.

"Come on, Rex." We head for the barn. I'm trying to figure out which animal could be sick. Hank's got Starlight out in the pasture. That leaves the two young horses he's been training.

Or Blackfire.

Before Dakota showed up at the Rescue, the black gelding was called Black Devil, and he lived up to the name. Old Mrs. Coolidge got him at an auction because she knew that if she didn't, the buyer would turn the horse into horse meat or dog food. Hank worked with the horse, but it wasn't going so good. For once, Hank's horse magic wasn't doing the job.

Then Dakota showed up. She and Blackfire took to each other, and they've been together ever since.

Rex and I squeeze through the side door of the barn. Right away it's obvious the vet's here for Blackfire. Dakota has the horse tied to a post in the round pen she and Hank use for training. Even this far away, I can see she's been crying.

"What's the matter with Blackfire, Doc?" Dakota asks. She's holding her horse by the halter, positioning herself between Blackfire and the vet, probably so the gelding won't take a chunk out of the vet's back while he's bent over.

Tri-County Animal Clinic is run by three vets—two women and this guy, Doc Jim. He's small, wiry, and strong as a pit bull. Blackfire keeps trying to jerk his front hoof away, but Doc manages to keep it up.

"I'm almost done, Dakota," he says.

46

Dakota Brown is 16, pretty, with black, curly hair and big brown eyes. I don't think she notices, but guys do double takes when she walks by. She could pass for an Indian, or Native American, whatever you call it.

I've known a lot of kids who've grown up in foster care. Nobody tells a straight story about "before"–what their lives were really like *before* foster care. Dakota told me that she had a brother who was killed in the war and then her mother died because she couldn't deal. And then her dad died because he couldn't live without his wife. It's a good story, but too made-for-TV. I let her get away with it, but I guarantee things didn't go down the way she says they did *before*.

I can't read Dakota the way Rex reads me. But right now it's pretty clear she's fighting to keep herself together.

Doc Jim lets go of Blackfire's hoof, and even I can tell the horse isn't putting much weight on that leg.

I move up to the pen and lean over the top rail. Dakota doesn't seem to know that me and Rex are there until Doc nods our way.

"Hey, Wes," Doc calls. "How's the dog business?"

"Not bad," I answer.

Dakota ignores me. "Doc?" she asks, her voice filled with impatience. "What's the matter with my horse?"

"Well," Doc says, "I think it's an abscess, Dakota."

"An abscess?" Dakota sounds horrified. "On his hoof?"

Doc smiles at her and strokes Blackfire's shoulder. The horse backs away from him. "That's not so bad, really. Could have been a lot worse. We need to locate the abscess, though, and dig it out."

Tears seep from the corners of Dakota's eyes. I feel for her. But the vet said it's not so bad. At least the horse still has four legs. Not like the poor Pomeranian.

"How did it happen?" Dakota demands. "Is it my fault? I try to keep the stall clean, but I know I could do a better job. Maybe if I'd–"

Doc stops her. "It's not your fault. We're not even sure how horses get abscesses. Blackfire might have stepped on a stone or–"

"Because I rode him on the road?" Dakota's

face looks like someone slapped her. "Why did I have to do that? We have so much land to ride on, and I had to go out on the road."

"Dakota, it might not have been a stone," Doc Jim explains. "And even if it was, it wasn't your fault. I'm thinking the abscess is coming from inside, instead of outside."

"Are you saying Blackfire has sores *inside* of him? How can that happen? He's such a good horse." She hugs his neck, and her shoulders heave.

"Not like that," Doc explains. "Blackfire doesn't have sores inside. I meant that a change in feed or grass can get into the blood vessels and result in an infection. Pus forms and tries to push out through the hoof. Does that make sense? We just need to coax out the pus, the infection. Then we can treat it better. First, though, we've got to find the point of origin."

He digs into his doctor's bag and comes out with a silver instrument that looks like large wire cutters or blunt-end scissors. "Hold him, Dakota. But don't let him hurt you. If he rears up, get out of the way. I have to find out where the hoof's the most sensitive. He's not going to like this."

49

Doc's right about that. He presses the clipper thing into different spots on the horse's hoof. Blackfire flinches every time. I wonder if his whole hoof is bad.

I want to get a better look, but I don't want to go inside the pen. I don't trust that black horse. As a rule, I stick with dogs and have as little to do with the horses as possible.

Doc Jim presses the silver thing on one side of the hoof. Blackfire lets loose a squeal and jerks back. Doc drops the hoof. "Guess we found the problem," he announces.

"Easy, boy." Dakota mumbles other things to her horse until he calms down. She strokes the sore leg all the way to the hoof. Then she lifts the hoof and nods for Doc to take over.

Doc slips in and takes the hoof from her, giving Dakota a weak smile.

"Go ahead, Doc," she says. "Do what you have to do. We're ready, aren't we, boy?" She stays close to Blackfire's head and leans her cheek against his.

Doc pulls a curved knife out of his pocket and goes to work. Strips of hoof fly to the ground. "I have to get as deep as I can," he tells Dakota.

He keeps digging.

Dakota winces with every slice of the knife, like she's the one getting cut.

Suddenly, Blackfire squeals and rears. Rex and I jump back. Even the vet backs away, pushing Dakota aside.

"I have to stop," Doc says. "I can't go any deeper."

"Did you get it?" Dakota asks. "The abscess?"

He shakes his head. "It's really in there deep. I could feel pus under the membrane. It's soft and squishy. But I don't want to go deeper."

Dakota swallows so hard that her neck quivers. "So how do we get it out?"

"You're going to have to soak the hoof in Epsom salts a couple times a day to draw the infection out of there." Doc studies Dakota. "You think you can do that?"

She nods and scratches Blackfire under his mane.

I, personally, can't even picture this. Soak that horse's hoof? I wouldn't touch that hoof with a 10-foot leash.

Doc gives her more instructions. "Soak the

hoof for as long as you can each time. Shoot for 20 minutes. Twice a day."

Right on cue, in walks Hank, leading Starlight. "I didn't know you were here, Doc," he calls from the doorway. "I thought you weren't coming by until later."

"I juggled a few things and got here early," Doc says. "Dakota sounded pretty desperate." Doc grins at Dakota, but she doesn't give it back.

Hank leads his horse toward her stall. "Just a minute—I'll be right back." When he returns a minute later, he's carrying his saddle. He chucks it into the tack room and jogs over to us. "So, what's the verdict?"

Hank makes the vet go through the whole diagnosis and treatment again. What's he think? That Dakota and I are idiots? That he's the only one who can do anything around here?

Rex nudges me. I know he'll start barking any minute if I let big-brother Hank get to me. I reach over and scratch my dog's chest and behind his ears until both of us calm down again.

"I'll go ahead and give Blackfire a shot of penicillin now," Doc says, digging the syringe out of his bag. "Can you give him another shot tomorrow, Hank? Saturday too, just to be on the safe side."

"No problem."

Hank helps Doc steady Blackfire for the first shot. Doc Jim keeps the syringe behind his back, pats the horse's neck, flicks a spot with his finger, then slips in the syringe.

Blackfire whinnies and jerks his head up, but he's better than I thought he'd be.

I wait around while Hank walks Doc to his truck. Then I clear my throat and ask, "You okay, Dakota?"

"No. How would you be if your dog had an abscess?"

I don't take the bait. Dakota and I got off to a bad start, and we haven't exactly *bonded* since. People expect fosters to act like brothers and sisters, but we're not.

I knew from day one that Dakota Brown was planning on running away from here. I could see it in her eyes. I could hear it in what she wasn't saying. Didn't matter to me. In fact, I would have been glad to see her go.

She planned her getaway perfectly, and she almost pulled it off. She would have too, if I hadn't given her away and told everybody what she was up to. I'm still not sure why I stopped her. But since then, she's fit in better than me around this place.

Dakota leans her head against her horse's shoulder. "Maybe I did something wrong. I'm no horse whisperer. Not like Hank. Or Winnie."

Winnie again. Winnie the Horse Gentler is famous around here, even though I've never seen her. She lives in Ohio and hangs with Hank's cousin, a guy they call Catman. They don't have an animal rescue, but they're into animals like we are. Hank and Dakota e-mail Winnie for horse advice, like she's this big horse genius.

"I heard Doc say it wasn't your fault. Besides, nobody else could ride that horse." Two months ago Dakota hadn't even ridden a horse. Now she rides Blackfire bareback at an all-out gallop.

She hugs Blackfire's neck. "Guess I won't be riding for a long time, will I, Blackfire?"

"You won't be riding?"

"Not hardly."

I hadn't thought of that. I wasn't even going to bother asking Dakota to help me with the dogs. She spends every minute with the horses. But if she isn't riding Blackfire, then she'll have more free time.

"Listen," I begin, "since you're going to have extra time on your hands, I just picked up four dogs from the pound, and—"

"Extra time? Are you kidding? I'm going to spend every minute of every day with my horse until he's well."

"You can't be here every minute."

"What would you know about it?" She spits the words at me. "You have no idea what it's like to have an animal need you and—"

"Are you crazy? I've got five dogs depending on me. Five! Not one."

"I can't believe you're trying to dump this on me!" Dakota shouts. "Never mind that my horse can't even put weight on one leg."

"Your horse is going to be fine." I heard the vet say so, and so did she. "At least he *has* four legs. My Pom—"

"Me, me, me! It's always all about Wes, isn't it?" Dakota screams.

My heart is slamming in my chest. Why did I even try to talk to her? "Just forget it. I'm sorry I said anything."

Rex is barking. He springs at my leg, then bounces down.

"Sorry?" Dakota says. "Even Rex knows that's a lie. You're not sorry. You're angry."

I can't argue with that. Now I *am* angry. "Dakota Brown, I should have let you run away."

SIX

DINNER IS A NOISY EVENT at the Coolidge table. Dr. Annie quizzes us during the whole meal. I think she's afraid that while she was in town doing surgery, she may have missed something really important on the farm.

"Hank," Annie prods, "how are the two young horses coming along?" She's sitting so close to Popeye that I don't know how either of them can eat. But they do. Dr. Annie isn't skinny. She's shaped kinda like a bowling pin.

Once Annie and Popeye dragged Kat and me to a carnival. The whole scene was pretty lame, except for this loud dude who guessed people's weight or what they did for a living. Annie wouldn't let the guy weigh her, so he tried to guess her line of work. He examined her hands, studied her up and down. Then he took a stab at what Annie Coolidge did for a living. He guessed grocery store clerk, elementary school teacher, and homemaker before Popeye proudly told the little crowd that had gathered that his wife was a surgeon.

The guy busted out laughing. He turned to Popeye and said, "And I'll bet you're a rocket scientist."

Annie was the one who set him straight. "Much more important than that," she told the guy. "My husband is a fireman."

When Annie talks, Popeye stares at her, like every word matters. He hands her the butter for her third biscuit the instant she finishes her second.

Hank takes another bite of the tuna casserole Popeye threw together. "I saddled both of the new horses, but I haven't mounted either of them yet. They're too skittish. Starlight and I went for a long ride instead. I almost missed Doc Jim."

All eyes zero in on Dakota, who hasn't

said two words during the meal. Neither have I, although I don't think anybody noticed. Kat didn't come down for dinner, so it's pretty much been a Coolidge conversation so far.

"Dakota," Popeye says, "tell my Annie about the doc's visit."

Dakota twists the napkin in her lap. I don't think she's eaten anything. "The vet didn't really do much. Blackfire's got an abscess in his hoof, and Doc Jim couldn't get it out. He couldn't even get it to drain. He just kept cutting and cutting, but it didn't do any good." She stops and swallows, but I'm pretty sure she's swallowing tears and not casserole.

Hank jumps to the vet's defense. "Doc Jim did everything he could. He cut into the hoof until he couldn't go deeper. He thinks soaking Blackfire's hoof will make the abscess drain. And the penicillin should keep the infection down."

"That makes sense," Popeye says. Then, just like he's talking to one of us, he prays, eyes open, no change in his voice. "Father, we ask You to take care of Blackfire for us. Help Dakota know what to do. Comfort both of them. Thanks for that horse and the way he's been coming around. Pass the biscuits, please."

The last part he aims at me. I pass the biscuits.

Annie and Popeye keep the conversation going. But I concentrate on getting dinner down so I can walk the dogs before it gets too dark.

"Wes," Annie says, scooping up another helping of casserole, "I stopped at Nice Manor today, and George was there. She said the residents can't wait to see the dogs you've got for them."

I've never heard anybody except Annie call Georgette Coolidge "George."

"I've got a lot of training to do with the dogs before they're ready for the nursing home," I say, finishing off my last green bean. It's not going to be easy to teach that bulldog not to jump up on people.

"Assisted living," Annie corrects. "Better not let the residents hear you calling Nice Manor a nursing home. There's a big difference. Nobody will be bedridden or needing constant nursing care. Then again, George was saying that if this pet program works for the hardier residents, she thinks it will work at Nice Nursing Home. Those people would love having animals around."

Annie takes a bite, chews, and dabs her lips with her napkin. "I do hope someone will like the dog with three legs." Before dinner Annie gave each dog a checkup, and I knew she took to the Pom. "All four dogs are really quite fit, considering where they come from. They could stand to put on weight, except for that peculiar-looking dog that kept jumping on me."

"I'll fatten 'em up in no time," I promise.

Above us, the Pomeranian's toenails *click-click* as he walk-hops, pacing my bedroom floor.

"Can I go walk the dogs now?" I ask, getting up from the table.

"I suppose," Annie says.

"Wait!" Dakota tosses her napkin on her plate, covering her uneaten food. "What about dishes? It's Wes's turn to wash."

"It's going to be dark if I wait any longer," I explain.

Beside me, Rex, who's been lying at my feet, sits up.

"You should have thought of that before dinner," Dakota says.

"Thought of what?" I snap. "When they gotta go, they gotta go. Nothing to think about. Since nobody's going to help me walk the dogs, what am I supposed to do?"

"The dishes." Dakota leans back in her chair and folds her arms in front of her. "I'm sure not doing them."

"Because you have so much to do?" I shove my chair in, but it slides too hard and slams the table. Rex starts barking.

"I'm e-mailing Winnie to ask her how to soak Blackfire's hoof, not that it's any of your business. And I have to check on my horse. So, yeah. I *do* have a lot to do."

"Yeah. Must be rough taking care of one animal," I say, pouring on the sarcasm. "*One*. And you don't even have to walk him."

"Well, you don't—"

"That's enough," Popeye says.

Dakota stops, but if looks had volume, hers would be earsplitting.

"Say, my love," Annie says, as she stands up and gathers their plates, "how would you like to cuddle with me over a sink of dirty dishes?"

"There's no place I'd rather be," Popeye answers.

"Fine," Dakota mumbles. "Do Wes's job for him." She gets up, drops her dishes into the sink, and heads outside.

I start with the littlest dog first. After 20 minutes with the Pom, I've learned two facts about him: (1) He can get around better on three legs than some dogs do on four. And (2) he takes his sweet time doing his business.

The terrier isn't much better. Every little sound throws her off. Just when I think she's finally going to do what we're out here for, she hears Dakota slamming things in the barn or Annie and Popeye laughing from the kitchen or a cricket chirping. And it's a no go.

By the time I get done with all the dogs, it's dark. Popeye, Annie, Hank, and Dakota are stretched out on the grass for a moon check. Almost every night, unless it's raining, we check out the night sky. I thought it was pretty lame at first, but it's okay. Popeye knows the names of the stars, and he can point out a million constellations.

"Hurry, Wes!" Popeye hollers. "You don't want to miss the show tonight."

"Be out in a minute," I answer.

I kennel the Blab and the bulldog but leave

63

the kennel doors open. Then I dash upstairs to check on the Pom and the terrier. I find them curled up together in the dog bed.

I ease the door shut so I don't disturb them. Then I head back toward the stairway.

Dakota's bedroom door is open, and the light's on. Annie hates it when we leave the lights on. Besides, Dakota's room faces the front of the house. Even the little bit of light from her window can cut down on our sky view.

I step into her room and start to turn off her light when I see something that gets my attention. My name. There's a piece of paper on Dakota's dresser, and my name is on it. From where I'm standing, still in the doorway, it looks like some kind of list.

Dakota is famous for her lists. Sometimes she writes down "to do" lists or "to get" lists. Mostly, she lists things in her journal. But this one's lying out in plain sight. And that's *my* name I'm looking at.

It's not like this is her private journal. I'd never touch one of her real journals. This is definitely different. This list is out in the open for anybody to read. I mean, her door was open. The light was on. Plus, *Wes* is on that list.

In two strides, I'm at Dakota's dresser. I don't touch her list, but I read:

TOP 10 TIPS FOR TAKING CARE OF BLACKFIRE
1. Use an old feed bucket for the water.
2. Make the water warm, not too cold or too hot.
3. Play music while you soak the hoof.
4. Scratch his withers during the process.
5. Start and finish with a handful of oats.
6. Don't soak the hoof the same time he gets his shot.
7. Keep the stall clean and dry.
8. Hang out with him after the soaking.
9. Pray.
10. WES–Keep him as far away from my horse, and me, as possible.

Real nice. I turn off the light and go downstairs.

SEVEN

"WES, COME TAKE A LOOK AT THIS," Hank calls. He scoots over, making room for me between him and Annie.

This is where Kat usually sits, and I don't like taking her spot. I want to know what's wrong with her this time, why she's sleeping so much. But I don't ask. Maybe I don't really want to know.

Finally, I plop onto her spot because it's better than where I usually sit, on the end next to Dakota. The air is still sticky hot, but it's the coolest it's been all week. I hope it cools down before my mom gets out of rehab. She hates the heat.

Dakota is talking to Popeye. "Winnie e-mailed me some tips on how to pull off soaking Blackfire's hoof. I plan to use that old feed bucket from the tack room. Winnie says music should help keep Blackfire calm, so I'm borrowing Kat's iPod docking station to play music out in the barn."

She keeps babbling, and I recognize other tips that were on that list in her room. I should have known she got them from Winnie the Horse Gentler. All except the last item on her list, the one about me. Thinking about it makes my stomach ball up into a fist.

Rex trots up and sits next to me. His ears are back. I don't want him to bark and give away how angry I am at Dakota. I lean back and stare through tree branches at a sky full of stars. Rex lies down too. It's an average sky night. The moon is three-quarters, so its light wipes out the Milky Way. On some winter nights, the sky looks like a black sheet full of pinpricks, with light leaking through from the other side.

"Are you looking?" Hank asks me.

"I'm looking," I tell him.

"Sirius," Hank says.

"I'm serious," I promise.

Dakota laughs.

Annie speaks up. "The name of that bright star is Sirius. S-i-r-i-u-s."

Dakota snorts out another dry laugh.

"Sirius is the brightest star in the northern hemisphere tonight. We'll be able to see it better in January though," Hank explains.

Right. Like I'll still be here in January. "And I care about this star because . . . ?"

Rex's tail slams the grass, back and forth. He barks twice. I stroke him, and he stops.

Hank sits up and frowns at me. "Because another name for Sirius is 'the Dog Star.' It's part of Canis Major. The Big Dog. Dad can make out the whole constellation, but I can just figure out pieces of it. Until December or January anyway."

I kinda like that there's a dog star. I squint up at the sky, but I can't see anything that looks like a dog.

Popeye moves over by me and puts his head next to mine so we're looking at the same thing. "There." He points at the brightest star in the sky. "That's the Dog Star. Now, those two stars above it are the shoulder and the eye of the Big Dog constellation." His chubby finger traces the air, like he's drawing on the sky. "Over there's the nose. Below, you can make out two front paws. Then go back there, and that's a hind leg, and two stars for the tail. Pretty soon we'll get the Little Dog, too."

I really do try to see what Popeye sees. I make out some of the stars he's pointing to, but that's it. "Popeye, you know I can't fill in the blanks on this sky stuff."

"Use your imagination!" Annie cries. Her voice makes the command sound like song lyrics. "I think the Big Dog resembles that skinny beagle you brought home from the shelter."

I gaze at the stars and try again, but it's a no go. No beagles in my sky. I shake my head. "Nothing."

"Try again, Wes," Hank urges, getting a little too big brotherly. "You know how people talk about the dog days of summer? The Egyptians used to blame the Dog Star for the extra heat in summer. They figured it had to come from the brightest star in the sky, the Dog Star."

"Give it up," Dakota advises. "Wes doesn't care about any of that. He just cares about his own little world."

I've about had it with her. "Like you don't?"

"I'm thinking about my horse. Not myself," she says.

"Right. The big soaking plan. If you ask me, it's all one big excuse to hang out in the barn all day. Or e-mail Winnie the Great Horse Gentler."

"Winnie's helping me take care of Blackfire!" Dakota shouts.

"That's right." My sarcasm is picking up steam now. "I'll bet Winnie helped with your mighty list. Was it her idea to keep Wes as far away as possible?"

Dakota springs to her feet. "You read my journal!"

"Did not!" I get to my feet too. I didn't touch her stupid journal.

"You did so!" she screams. "You were in my room!"

"You left the light on, like always!" I shout back.

"So I left the light on. So what? You're not my mother."

"Who'd want *that* job?"

We charge at each other until we're nose to nose.

"Get out of my face, Dakota!" I warn.

"Make me!" she shouts back.

"That'll be enough." Popeye wedges his round body between us. "No more. You two have been at each other all day. This ends here."

"But he–"

"She's been–"

"No more." Popeye says it quietly. Calmly. But his words have force. "I've come up with a punishment and a solution." He grins at Annie, who smiles back.

This can't be good.

Popeye turns to Dakota. "Dakota, Wes needs your help with these dogs. You're going to help him."

Dakota explodes. "That's not fair! I have Blackfire to take care of."

"Very true," Popeye answers softly. He turns to me. "Which is why Wes here will be happy to help you with your horse."

EIGHT

FRIDAY MORNING I wake up before the sun, thanks to the Pom licking my face.

"Take it easy, man," I say, lifting him off my chest. "Leave some skin, will you?" Then it hits me. "Hey, how did you get up here?"

The Pom strains to get at my face again with his long tongue. I can't figure how he did it, but he must have jumped up on my bed during the night.

Rex is lying beside my bed, like he has every night since I found him. I reach down and stroke his head. His tail goes *thwack, thwack* against the floor.

I drag myself out of bed and set the Pom next to Rex. "Where's your buddy?"

It takes some searching, but I find the terrier cowering under my bed. "Come on out, girl," I beg. "Aren't you hungry? Want to go for a walk?"

That gets through to her. She crawls out and huddles beside the Pomeranian. I tuck one dog under each arm like footballs and head out with Rex tagging behind.

As soon as I open my bedroom door, I hear the two kenneled dogs barking on the front porch. They're ready too. No way I can take all five dogs at the same time.

Kat, still in her nightgown, sticks her head out of her bedroom. She hasn't put on a wig, so the tiny, white fuzz on her bald head catches the light from the hall. "Wes?" She rubs her eyes and yawns. "Everything okay?"

"It's cool, Kat," I tell her. "Under control. Just walking the dogs."

She looks like she should still be in bed. Sometimes I get scared that she'll fall down and break into pieces. But that's just the outside. Inside, that kid is 10 times stronger than any of us. When the social worker first dropped me off at Starlight, I was fighting mad at the whole world. I wouldn't talk to anybody—not Ms. Bean (the social worker), not any of the Coolidges, and not the little white girl who trailed me everywhere I went. But Kat kept following me anyway, telling me about all the kittens she was taking care of, filling me in on Hank and Annie and Popeye. She talked about God, too, although I don't remember what she said. Just that she talked about God different than most other people do. Like He's not as far away as you think. I lived on the farm two whole weeks before I knew Kat was sick.

"Need any help?" she asks, yawning again.

"Nah. I got it." I set the terrier down and snap on her leash. "You go back to bed."

Kat grins and slips into her room. I'd probably never say it out loud, but I'm going to miss that kid when I move back in with my mom.

The terrier won't go down the stairs on her leash, and I don't think the three-legged Pomeranian can handle the steep steps. So I end up carrying both dogs downstairs.

Dr. Annie is sipping a cup of tea at the table. Next to her, Popeye, chin in hands, stares at his wife like he's memorizing her face.

"Morning, Wes. Looks like you've got your hands full," Annie says.

"You think?" I return.

Popeye grins at me, and I know what's coming. A joke. Bad, as only he can tell it. "Say, Wes, what happened to the dog that ate too much garlic?"

I learned a long time ago that the best way to get through Popeye's jokes is fast. Like ripping off a Band-Aid. "Don't know," I say, like I *need* to know this answer.

"What happened to the dog that ate too much garlic?" Popeye always repeats his joke before answering it himself. "His bark really was worse than his . . . bite!" He breaks out laughing before he gets the last word out.

"Good one," I say, without enthusiasm.

Annie elbows him. "One more, sweetheart. Please?"

I give her the evil eye, but she's not looking at me. Her gaze is on Popeye.

"Well," he says, "if you insist. What do you get when you cross a dog and a lion?"

He raises his bushy eyebrows at me, so I have to play along. It's the only way to get him to quit. "I don't know."

"What do you get when you cross a dog and a lion? A terrified postman." Popeye and Annie laugh so hard they fall into each other's arms.

The two dogs on the porch start barking like crazy again. Rex trots to the door and presses his nose to the screen.

I stand in the middle of the kitchen, not sure which dog or dogs to walk first.

"Where's Dakota?" Annie asks.

"How should I know?" I answer. "Probably sleeping."

"She better get up," Popeye says, clearing their dishes.

Annie walks her cup to the sink. She's wearing khaki pants with an elastic waist. Her pink shirt is stuffed into the waistband. "Want me to wake Dakota for you, Wes?"

"For *me*?" I don't get it. Then I remember. Dakota has to help me with the dogs. "Cool! Do it, Annie."

I stay downstairs with the dogs and Popeye, although I'd love to see the scene in Dakota's room. Turns out I hear parts of it, especially the end.

"Fine!" Dakota shouts.

"I thought you'd feel that way," Annie says

sweetly. I hear footsteps on the stairs. Then Annie appears. "Dakota will be right down. As for me, I've got to get to the hospital."

"Must you?" Popeye sounds desperate.

"'Fraid so, my love," Annie says.

We go through this every morning. I think they've been married 20 years.

Annie pats her pockets. Then she dashes to the table, then over to the sink and back to the computer. Finally, she reaches into her pocket and comes out with her car keys. "There they are." She whizzes past me, with Popeye on her heels. "Bye-bye."

"Bye," I call after her.

She gets as far as the screen door, then turns and races back to the kitchen. "Has anybody seen my purse?"

Popeye retrieves the giant black bag. "Here you are, my Annie." He kisses her hand and walks her out to the minivan.

Through the screen I watch as Popeye opens the car door for Annie. When she drives off, he waves and keeps waving, even after the van's out of view and the dust has settled.

It's pretty wack. But I admit I wouldn't mind someone caring about my mom like that.

The Pom squirms to get down and out of my arms. Rex nudges the screen, wanting out. The kenneled dogs are barking, demanding their freedom.

I holler toward the stairs, "Dakota, hurry up!"

These dogs aren't going to wait much longer. I find the leashes and head for the porch. The sun is rising. If I wasn't so sleepy, it would be pretty cool out here. A red streak swirls below a bank of clouds. In Chicago, it was hard to see over the projects to the sky. Or maybe I wasn't looking.

Finally, Dakota stumbles out to the porch. I'm guessing she slept in the shorts and T-shirt she's wearing. Her hair is smushed on one side and frizzy on the other.

"Nice outfit," I say. "Great hair."

"Shut up and give me a dog," Dakota replies.

I take Rex and the Pom for the first round of walks. The two dogs hit it off. Rex lags back for the Pom, and the three-legged guy shows a lot of spunk trying to keep up. I let them both off the leash on the way back to the house.

Dakota starts out with the Blab. He's a

handful. All he wants to do is play. Play with his leash, play with Dakota's untied shoelaces, play with leaves on the ground. But Dakota sticks with it. We don't say a word to each other. But together we get all five dogs walked and fed before Hank's finished working his first horse.

"You didn't do so bad," I tell her when we finally go back in.

"I like dogs," she admits. "Not as much as horses, but dogs aren't bad."

I hang up the leashes in the porch, where I've screwed in hooks.

Dakota walks to the kitchen. When I get there, she's pulling a note off the fridge. "Popeye says he's driving Kat to town and won't be back until suppertime."

She sets the note on the counter, and I read it for myself. "You think he took her to the hospital?"

"No. He would have said. She's not due for more chemo for a while either." Dakota gets out the oatmeal.

I pop two pieces of bread into the toaster and get out the peanut butter.

We're quiet while each of us fixes our own breakfast.

"Do you think Kat's getting any better?" Dakota asks. She pulls a stool up to the counter, where I'm already eating my toast.

I shrug. "I don't know. She's been sleeping a lot lately."

"I've been praying for her," she says. "It helps *me*. I just hope it's helping Kat."

I don't know what to say, so I don't say anything.

"Do you pray, Wes?"

I get up and pour myself a glass of milk. "Sometimes. Kind of." I down the whole glass standing up, then set the cup in the sink. I don't want to talk about praying or Kat. I'm too tired to even think about how sick Kat is.

A yawn comes from way inside of me, and I let it out. I didn't get much sleep last night with three dogs in my room. "Dakota, I'm beat. Thanks for the help. I'm going back to bed. If Hank comes in, tell him to keep it down, okay?"

"No. *Not* okay." Dakota walks over to me and gets in my face. "You're not going anywhere, Wes."

"Excuse me? Who died and made you boss? I'm going back to bed. Deal with it,

Dakota." I like the sound of that. I picture a bumper sticker with the slogan: *Deal with it, Dakota.* Man, I really *am* tired.

I make a move to go around her, but she blocks me.

"Wesley Williams, the only place you're going is to the barn. You and I have a date with Blackfire."

NINE

"HAVE I TOLD YOU LATELY how glad I am you're not my real sister?" I ask Dakota.

"Feeling's mutual," Dakota assures me.

This is our fourth trip to the barn. We've carried out enough salt and water to start our own ocean.

"Go ahead and dump that small bag of salts into the trough. Then mix it up really well," she orders. "I'll go get Blackfire. Better keep your distance when I bring him out."

"Don't have to tell me twice. That wild animal looks like he wants to stomp me."

"He's a very intelligent horse," Dakota comments. She jogs off to Blackfire's stall.

I can't believe Hank's not around to help. I shove the black rubber feed bucket, filled with warm water, closer to the pole. I'm pretty sure that's where Dakota will tie her horse. The trough is about a foot and a half deep. I dump in the salt and slosh it around with a stick until I hear Blackfire and Dakota coming.

Dakota leads Blackfire to the round pen. He's limping worse than yesterday. "Is everything ready, Wes?" she calls.

"I guess." I hustle out of the pen, leaving the gate open for her.

When she leads Blackfire in, the horse lays back his ears. Even I know that's not a great sign. I know what angry looks like.

I station myself a safe distance outside the pen. I wish I had Rex with me, but Dakota made me leave him in the house. She was afraid Rex would pick up on my anger and bark, scaring Blackfire.

First, Dakota brushes her horse, smoothing his coat after each stroke. She starts with the head and works her way back. Then she moves around to the other side and does the whole routine all over again.

I think she's dragging this out just to drive me crazy. It's working. "C'mon, Dakota. Blackfire looks clean to me."

"He *is* clean." She drags the brush down each foreleg and up again. "I'm not brushing Blackfire because he's dirty. Touching him is part of the bonding process."

"No kidding? That's what I do with dogs."

When I found Rex by the side of the road and carried him back to the farm, he was so weak that he couldn't raise his head. But I could feel him tremble with fear. For the first 48 hours, all I did was pet him. Something about touching him made me feel a part of Rex, and it worked the same way for him. I didn't even know you called it "bonding" until Hank told me.

Dakota keeps brushing her horse. "Winnie says the more I stroke Blackfire before soaking his hoof, the calmer he'll be. . . . I almost forgot. Turn on the music."

She's already got the iPod and docking station plugged in and ready to go. All I have to do is punch the button. I'm expecting elevator music or something you'd hear at the dentist's office, but what comes out of the speakers is jazz. Not bad.

"You should e-mail Barker on the Pet Helpline, Wes. Winnie says Eddy Barker knows as much about dogs as she knows about horses or Catman knows about cats. I'll bet Barker could give you some tips about training dogs for Nice Manor."

"Rex taught me everything I need to know about dogs." I wish she'd get off my back. I don't need help from Barker or anybody.

Dakota sets down the brush. "Okay. Your turn."

"Yeah, right."

"Get in here, Wes!" she snaps.

I stay where I'm at. "What? Did you forget your own list? 'Keep Wes away from Blackfire'?"

"I don't have time for this, Wes." Dakota keeps her voice soft, no doubt so she doesn't scare her horse. But her words are forced through bared teeth. "Look, if you brush him, maybe he'll let you help me. *Get . . . in . . . here.*"

I shake my head. "I'm not touching that horse."

"Fine." She glares at me. "Don't touch

him. But get close enough so he can get used to you, at least."

I enter the pen and get close enough to see the whites of his eyes.

"Closer," Dakota whisper-shouts.

I move closer.

Dakota holds out the brush to me.

"I told you I'm not touching that horse."

"You don't have to touch him, you coward. Just brush him."

I should walk out right now. Nobody calls me a coward. But I need her to help with the dogs. "Give me the stupid brush," I mutter.

"Take it." She shoves the brush at me.

I take it. Then I hold out the brush and move in until the bristles touch Blackfire's neck.

His neck quivers, like a fly landed on it. The horse flinches.

I drop the brush and run for the gate.

"Wes, get back here!" Dakota shouts.

I stop running and turn around. Blackfire paws the dirt. He's not rearing or anything. He's tied up. "Okay. But keep him still, will you?"

Dakota sighs.

I try again. This time he lets the brush

touch his neck, and he doesn't freak out on me. Still, I stand as far from the horse as possible.

"Brush him!" Dakota whispers.

I move the brush down his neck and shoulder. He lets it happen. After a few strokes, I feel the tension seep out of him. I breathe again. On the iPod, jazz shifts into blues. At least Dakota didn't do too bad with the tunes.

"Keep doing what you're doing," Dakota instructs. "I need to pick his hoof before I soak it." She pulls a hoof pick out of her back pocket, eases in next to the gelding's shoulder, and picks up the bad hoof. "Easy, boy," she coos.

I move behind her and keep brushing while Dakota picks dirt and straw from the hoof.

"It still hasn't drained," she complains.

I stop brushing and stand where I can see better. When the hoof pick reaches the sore spot, Blackfire jerks his hoof away. It hits the ground an inch from Dakota's foot.

I'm halfway to the gate before Dakota yells, "Wes! Get back here!"

I go back, but I keep my distance this time. She has to start all over with the hoof pick. When she's done, she hands the pick to me without letting go of the hoof.

Slowly, she lets the horse's foreleg uncurl. She moves to the side and aims the hoof over the bucket. Blackfire flattens his ears. I jump out of the way.

In a flash, the horse jerks back. He pulls his hoof out of Dakota's hands and steps down into sawdust.

"Blackfire," Dakota scolds. But she doesn't raise her voice. She leans into his shoulder and lifts the hoof again. "Easy, boy," she says, while she digs out the sawdust. Then she tries again.

This time Blackfire lowers his hoof above the bucket. He paws the water once, then steps into it. His hoof misses the center of the bucket. Dakota struggles to get the hoof in better, but his weight squishes the side of the rubber bucket. Water seeps out, spilling onto sawdust, making a brown paste on the floor of the arena.

"This isn't working," Dakota complains. She wrestles with the foreleg until she gets the hoof up again. But by now, most of the water has drained out.

"Maybe we should wait for Hank," I suggest.

Dakota's head snaps up. "No. And why are you just standing there? Go get more hot water. And salt, too."

I hate having her boss me around, but I'm glad to get away from her horse. I take my time dragging out more salt and bringing another jug of water.

"Well, fill the bucket," Dakota says, her voice edgy. "I can't do everything."

"Yes, ma'am," I answer, sarcasm overflowing. I refill the bucket with salt and water, then step out of the way.

"No you don't," she says. "I need you here."

"And I need a house in the suburbs."

"I'm not kidding around." She's spraying words through clenched teeth again.

I move a little closer.

"Get over here!"

I move in so close I can smell horse sweat.

"When I give you the signal," she instructs, "push the bucket in. Got it?"

"Dakota–," I start.

"Do it, Wes," she commands. She lifts up the hoof and brushes the sawdust out. "Now."

I shove the bucket under the raised hoof and step back as fast as I can.

"Closer!" she commands.

"Man," I mutter. But I shove the bucket in closer.

Dakota eases the hoof into the bucket.

Blackfire starts to pull out his hoof, but Dakota is right there to guide it back to the bucket. "Come on, Blackfire," she urges, swaying under the weight of his hoof.

Blackfire paws at the water, then plunges his hoof squarely into the bucket.

"Good boy," Dakota coos, stroking the horse's neck. "That's it. This will help that soreness get out of you, baby."

Blackfire seems to settle into the water. His eyelids droop. His neck twitches, but he keeps his hoof in the salty water.

"Don't move," Dakota whispers to me. "Do you have a watch?"

I shake my head. Neither of us has a watch on, so we can't time the 20 minutes we're supposed to leave the hoof in the water. But Blackfire keeps his hoof in there so long, it's got to be at least that.

Finally, Dakota looks up at me. "Wes, we did it."

In that instant, Blackfire lifts his hoof, then drops it back into the bucket.

Water flies up and then streams down like some giant fountain. Before I can move, before I can back out of the way, the water rains down on me, splashing me, soaking me with a warm, salty, gross, horse-hoof bath.

TEN

EVEN AFTER FOUR SHOWERS, I still smelled like horse all day Friday. Over the next few days, though, Dakota and I find our groove. It takes less and less time to walk the dogs, so we have more time to hang out with them. We even figure out how to soak Blackfire's hoof without killing ourselves or each other.

Dakota stops being so bossy in the barn because I learn to read her horse and know what to do without her telling me. Whenever Blackfire is about to pull his hoof out of the bucket, he gives himself away by flattening his ears back. Then I grab the bucket, and Dakota strokes her horse's leg until he settles his hoof back in the salty water.

* * *

Tuesday morning I cross the day off my calendar, like always. Popeye and Annie gave me a dog calendar for Christmas, and August's dog of the month is a bulldog almost as ugly as our pound bulldog. As I make the big X on Tuesday, I can't believe we're almost there. Three more Xs to go, and Mom will have finished her 90 days in rehab. Ms. Bean, the social worker, promised to drive me to Chicago early enough so I can be there when Mom walks out on Saturday.

* * *

Tuesday night when we're outside for a moon check, Kat walks out with the phone. "Gram wants to talk to you." She shoves the phone at me.

Even in the dark I can feel everybody watching. "Hello?"

"Wesley?" It's definitely Mrs. Coolidge. She pronounces every letter in my name. I don't know how she does it. "I know you weren't planning on bringing your dogs to the Manor until Friday, but there's been a change of plans. I want you to introduce the dogs tomorrow."

"Tomorrow?" No way the bulldog can even be in the same room with old people, not until I teach her not to jump on them. The Blab still gets too excited around strangers. And the terrier will be scared out of her wits. "They're not ready yet."

"Nonsense. All you need to do is introduce the dogs and yourselves—I hear Dakota will be joining you."

"But—"

"I'll be by for you tomorrow afternoon. Don't keep me waiting." She hangs up before I can say anything. Nobody wins an argument with Georgette Coolidge.

✳ ✳ ✳

On Wednesday morning I get up so early I have to click on my bedside lamp to cross off the day on my calendar. The dogs are still asleep. Maybe that's why they call them "lucky dogs." I don't think I slept all night. I just stared at the ceiling and imagined the bulldog knocking down old people, one by one.

Then I switched mind channels and worried about my mom. I tried to figure out where Mom will live when she gets out of rehab. I have to take care of things, or somebody like T the Troll will move in on her. But I don't know how we'll pay the bills this time. Or when Mom will be ready for me to move back in with her. Or who will take care of the dogs when I'm gone.

Once, about 5 a.m., I imagined I saw Sirius the Dog Star on the ceiling. He was growling.

Dakota's not thrilled when I wake her up, but she stumbles downstairs and walks the dogs with me. When we're done, she helps me get them settled again on the porch. The sun is up, but just barely.

"Blackfire's probably still sleeping," she says, letting loose a noisier-than-it-needs-to-be yawn. "He's a lot smarter than some people around here." She yawns again, and it makes me yawn too. "We can soak Blackfire's hoof later. Mrs. C. said she wasn't coming until this afternoon, right?"

"Yeah."

"Then I'm going back to bed." She heads upstairs.

I start to follow her, then change my mind. I can't remember the last time I was the only one up in the morning at Starlight Animal Rescue. Maybe never.

I listen to the creak of the stairs and Dakota's footsteps overhead. Her door clicks open, then shut. From the other end of the house I hear Popeye snoring, or maybe Annie, or both. The kitchen's still smothered in garlic from last night's lasagna. There's the great musty smell of slightly wet dog, too. I breathe deep, remembering the stench of burning rubber from the plant behind the projects. This is better. Way better.

"Come on, Rex," I whisper, turning back to the kitchen. "Let's see if we can find an apartment online. One that doesn't stink. And loves dogs."

Rex wags his tail and follows me to the kitchen.

I grab a stale donut and sit down at the computer. Popeye set it up between the kitchen and dining room so he could keep an eye on us when we're online. Rex curls up at my feet and rests his head on my toes.

The computer's been left on. When I move the mouse, the screen lights up, and it's on the e-mail in-box. Instead of hitting the browser right away, I sit back and scan the list of e-mails. Dakota has a dozen exchanges with Winnie the Horse Gentler from the day before. Big surprise. But she's also got at least that many from Eddy Barker, the kid Hank calls a dog whisperer.

I'm not being nosy or reading her mail or anything. But the screen's right here, out in the open. I can't help it if I happen to read the messages.

Winnie,

Thanks for the tips on soaking Blackfire's hoof. You were right about everything. Yesterday I forgot the music, and Blackfire got restless and hard to handle. I was afraid he was going to splash Wes like he did the first day. Not that I couldn't use a good laugh like that again. But I'll be sure to remember the tunes tomorrow.

Okay. Here's what I need to know now: What if the abscess doesn't open up and drain? What if the infection backs up inside the bloodstream? Hank drove me to the Nice Library yesterday, and I checked out 11 books on horses (six on dogs). One of the horse health books said that this kind of infection can turn into something more serious.

Winnie, if anything happens to Blackfire, I don't think I could handle it. What if the abscess never breaks out? What if it keeps getting worse and worse? What if . . . What will I do then?

Dakota

I admit that I'd never thought about any of this. Dakota didn't tell *me* she was still scared for Blackfire.

I only meant to read Dakota's part of the e-mail. I wanted to see if she said anything about me to Winnie the Horse Gentler. But now I have to keep reading to see Winnie's answers about Blackfire's hoof.

Dakota,

Sorry things aren't going better with Blackfire. But it sounds like you and Wes are doing a great job. Wes isn't still angry with your horse for splashing him, is he? Of course Blackfire didn't mean anything by it.

As for the what-ifs, don't go there. You're doing everything you can do. Hank's giving the gelding penicillin. All that's left is for you to pray. Hey—God cares. He created that horse. He loves Blackfire even more than you do.

Praying with you, Winnie

P.S. Catman says to give a special "hey" to that groovy cat, Kat (his words, not mine). But you can tell Kat hi for me, too.

"Who are you writing, Wes?" Kat appears out of nowhere.

I wheel around to face her. She's carrying two of her cats, an orange tabby that's bigger than the Pomeranian and a dirty, white, scroungy cat named Kitten. "Didn't hear you come up, Kat."

"I figured, since you jumped liked a scared cat." She puts the cats outside, then pulls up a kitchen stool. Kat looks better than she has in days. She's wearing jeans, a red polo shirt, and her long blonde wig.

"You look okay," I tell her, scooting over so we can both see the screen.

"Wow. I'll bet you get lots of girls with that line." She grins and elbows me. "So, whose mail are you reading?"

"Stuff from the Pet Helpline. I was going to do some apartment hunting for Mom and me. Then I saw the e-mails."

"Anything from Barker? You and Eddy Barker ought to e-mail each other. He's so great with dogs."

Usually I hate it when anybody talks to me about how awesome Barker is with dogs. But right now, I guess I can use all the help I can get, even from Barker. I'd like a quick fix for the bulldog, for one thing. "Maybe I'll e-mail him," I tell Kat. "I'm pretty desperate. Mrs. Coolidge isn't giving me enough time to get the dogs ready for this thing. She's coming this afternoon."

"Gram's just excited. She thinks this is the best idea since sliced bread. It doesn't hurt that it's her idea. But I happen to agree with her."

I turn back to the screen and scroll through the horse messages until I get to some from Eddy Barker.

Dakota,

Winnie filled me in on how you're helping get dogs into the assisted-living home. As Catman would say, "Far out! Right on!" Did you know dogs can lower people's heart rates and blood pressure? Some insurance companies even give discounts for pet owners.

First, take a deep breath. You sound pretty fried. Don't worry about not being a "dog whisperer." There's no such thing as dog magic. People who are good with dogs just go with the dog's natural instincts. It helps to remember that dogs are pack animals. Every person and animal in the house—or the nursing home—will end up being part of the pack, whether they realize it or not. Dogs need to know where they stand, where their rank falls in the house. And life will go a lot smoother for everybody if the two-legged pack members outrank the four-legged ones. People need to be top dog.

So ask me anything you think could help. Fire away!

Barker

Dakota didn't waste any time taking Barker up on his offer:

Hey, Barker,

Thanks for doing this. Wes, the guy I'm helping with
the dogs, knows a lot about dogs. He's just not that
easy to talk to. I feel like it makes him mad when I
ask him too many questions. So I really appreciate
your help.

Dakota had followed that up with a list of
questions, and Barker had answered every one.

Only I stop reading the questions, and I
don't feel like reading any more answers.

"Why would she do that?" I mutter.

"Do what?" Kat asked.

"Go to this Barker kid to ask about dogs.
I know about dogs. She could have asked *me*.
Why would she say that? That I'm hard to talk
to? I don't get mad when she asks me questions." But I'm mad now. "She should have
asked me. Not some stranger."

ELEVEN

"DAKOTA DIDN'T MEAN ANYTHING BY IT," Kat says. "I think you're easy to talk to, Wes." She puts her small hand on my arm. If anybody else did that, I'd shake them off without a second thought.

But not Kat.

"You know what?" Kat says. "I was just about to ask you something about dogs myself. Like why they don't like cats more."

I give her my "yeah, right" look. But Kat makes it hard to stay mad. She also makes me wonder what it would have been like to have a sister. My mom never really wanted kids. One was more than enough for her.

"Do you want to help me search for an apartment in Chicago, or what?" I scoot my chair back, turning the keyboard over to Kat because we both know she's better at finding stuff online than I am. "Maybe we can find me a job, too, so I can pay the rent."

Kat glances at me. Her eyes are watery. She's known all along I'm going back to Chicago as soon as I can.

I clear my throat. "Apartments, Kat?"

"Okay." She clicks straight to a Web site that claims to specialize in "affordable" apartments. They're affordable, all right. As long as your name is Bill Gates or Trump, or maybe Michael Jordan.

"Try the south side of Chicago," I tell her. "See if they list apartments in the projects."

"I'll bet you could get a great job training dogs, Wes," Kat says. "Then you and your mom could get one of these apartments with a swimming pool. I'd come and visit."

"Try another site, Kat." I could never afford a place like that. But getting a job training dogs isn't a half-bad idea.

Kat surfs to a dozen different sites, but

106

even the cheapest apartment costs way more than Mom and I could ever afford.

"Maybe I should be looking for rooms to rent instead of apartments." No way that room above the bar cost this much. But places like that probably don't show up in cyberspace.

Kat squints at me. "When do you think you'll move away and live with your mom? I'm going to miss you, Wes."

Being missed isn't something I've counted on. Or missing. I'll miss Kat, even though I don't want to. "Not sure," I answer. "Guess I'll know more after I see Mom on Saturday."

"You must be so excited."

I glance back at the computer screen. "I was hoping to get some leads on an apartment before she gets out."

"I'll bet Ms. Bean can help," Kat suggests.

"Maybe." Ms. Bean's okay, for a social worker. But she never lived in the projects or over a bar.

"Morning!" Popeye calls, thundering downstairs. "You two are up mighty early." He sneezes.

"Bless you, Dad!" Kat calls.

"I am indeed blessed, my little Kat. And

so are you. Which reminds me of a joke." He heads for the fridge.

I grin because that's the funniest part of Popeye's jokes. Everything reminds him of a joke, but nobody else ever sees the connection.

"Which side of a dog has the most hair?" he asks, opening the fridge and staring inside.

Kat glides over to him and gives him her morning hug.

"Ah, that won't get you out of answering this riddle, Kat." He lifts her off the ground, hugs her, then sets her down.

"Wes?" Popeye grins at me. We both know I'm not the hugging kind.

I'm pretty sure I know the answer to his joke, even though I haven't heard the riddle before. But I won't spoil his morning. I shake my head and shrug. "Don't know."

"Which side of a dog has the most hair? The *out*side!" he shouts. "Get it?"

"We *all* get it." Dakota trudges down the stairs and stops behind Popeye. I try to wipe out of my mind what she said about me being hard to talk to. "Even the neighbors a mile over got it, Popeye."

"And top of the morning to you, Dakota,"

Popeye says. "I've got another one almost as good as that one. Why did the schnauzer—?" He breaks off in midquestion, tilts his head toward the stairs, then dashes to the foot of the stairs and gazes up as if he's waiting for the queen of England to strut down the red carpet. "My Annie!" he declares. "A vision of loveliness."

Annie shuffles down the stairs in her tan robe and fuzzy red slippers. Her hair is wound around plastic curlers. A couple of pink curlers dangle from the sides of her head like giant earrings. Wednesday is supposed to be her day off from the hospital, but it's pretty rare when she actually stays home the whole day. "Morning, all!"

Rex trots over to her and demands to be petted.

"How about if I make my special apricot pancakes?" she asks.

A second of silence passes. Annie Coolidge may be able to cook up miracle cures on her cancer ward, but she can't fry an egg without burning it.

"On your day off?" Popeye roars. "I won't hear of it."

"Popeye's right," Dakota agrees.

Kat and I grin at each other.

"You come sit here, my Annie, and rest those beautiful feet." Popeye pulls the chair out for her. "I'll whip up some chocolate chip pancakes. How'd that be?"

"You're too good for your own good, Mr. Coolidge," Annie says, taking the seat he holds out for her.

The screen door slams and in storms Georgette Coolidge, looking even taller than she actually is. Her long, bloodhound face would make her easy to pick out in a lineup. If the face didn't do it, then her hair would. It's blonde, but I'm guessing it didn't get that way on its own. Kat told me Mrs. Coolidge drives into Chicago every few days to get her hair done. She's wearing a light blue skirt and jacket that would fit perfectly in her parts of Chicago—downtown or the north side—but not *my* Chicago. And not out here.

"Mother!" Popeye runs to his mother and gives her a one-second hug. He's bald and she's blonde, but there's no doubt they're blood. "We weren't expecting you until this afternoon."

She raises her eyebrows at her son. "Sorry to disappoint, Chester."

"What? I-I-I didn't mean . . . I mean, we're glad you're here. Of course." He stammers and glances at Dr. Annie for help.

Annie strolls up to her mother-in-law. "You look lovely, George," she says. "Come on in."

"Wish I could." Mrs. Coolidge's back is so straight you could play pool on it. "But we're on our way to Nice Manor, aren't we, Wes and Dakota?"

Dakota drops her spoon. "Now?"

"Chill, Dakota. Mrs. Coolidge doesn't mean *now*," I say.

"*Now* means *now*," Mrs. Coolidge says evenly.

I haven't talked through the training plan with Dakota. I didn't get to brush the dogs after their walk. I need time to work with that bulldog. Plus, I wanted to get more information from Mrs. Coolidge about the Nice Manor residents. "Mrs. Coolidge, I need more time. I'll bet the Manor people need more time. Seriously, are you sure they're ready for us?"

"Wes is right, Mrs. Coolidge," Dakota

agrees. For once, she's on my side. "Are you sure they're expecting us this early?"

"Not at all!" Mrs. Coolidge exclaims. A tiny smile creeps onto her bright red lips. "That will be half the fun."

TWELVE

KAT HELPS US GET THE DOGS TO THE CAR. Popeye helps me carry the kennels. We're still only using two kennels because I don't have the heart to put the Pomeranian or the frightened terrier into cages again.

Dakota climbs in front. Mrs. Coolidge doesn't allow animals in the front seat of her new car, even though the car's big enough for a couple of horses, so that leaves me in back with all the dogs.

"Mrs. C.," Dakota reasons, "don't you think we should at least call the activities director and tell her we're on our way?"

"No, sirree," Mrs. Coolidge answers. "We don't want to give them fair warning."

"But it's all set up, isn't it?" I ask. "I mean, they know we're coming. They're up for this pilot pet program, aren't they?"

She doesn't answer.

"Mrs. Coolidge?" I press. "They want our dogs, don't they?"

"Well, not exactly. Not yet," she admits. "Consider this an audition. A tryout."

"You've got to be kidding," Dakota says.

"Oh, for goodness' sake," Mrs. Coolidge says. "Don't be such a worrywart. The board at Nice Manor approved our pet project, although they left the details to their activities director." She adjusts her air-conditioning vent, even though she hasn't turned on the AC yet. "The problem is their activities director. As soon as she found out I was behind the project, she got cold feet. I'm afraid Miss Golf and I have a history."

This can't be good. Mrs. Coolidge should have told us before now. "What if nobody's there to meet the dogs?" I ask.

The woman shoots me a frown in the rearview mirror. "It's all under control," she says. "I have an inside man."

"An inside man?" Dakota repeats.

"Woman, actually," Mrs. Coolidge clarifies. "Her name is Buddy, and she's got spunk. Believe me, our Miss Golf is no match for Buddy."

I don't ask anything else, and neither does Dakota. I'm trying to picture an inside woman with spunk who goes by the name of Buddy. It's enough to keep me busy until we get there.

Nice Manor is set back from the road and surrounded by trees. The brick building isn't a skyscraper or anything, but there must be at least five stories. Hard to believe this is an old people's home. They probably fix up the outside and leave the inside junky.

"Out you go!" Mrs. Coolidge commands.

"You're not coming?" Dakota sounds terrified.

"Places to go, people to see," Mrs. Coolidge explains.

I have to hang on to the Pomeranian so he won't bolt out of the car when Dakota opens the door. The terrier acts like she's glued to my thigh, but I wrestle her loose and hand her to Dakota. The other dogs are banging to get out of their kennels. Dakota leashes the terrier and the Blab while I juggle the Pom and the bulldog.

Mrs. Coolidge taps the steering wheel. "Call my cell when you're ready to be picked up."

Dakota and I back away from the car, our dogs straining at the leashes. I feel like I did the first time I was dropped off at a foster home.

Before she drives away, Mrs. Coolidge rolls down her window and calls out, "Get along, little doggies!"

We don't move. I couldn't wave good-bye if I wanted to. And I don't want to. This whole thing is her fault.

Mrs. Coolidge honks her horn twice, then peels out of the parking lot, leaving Dakota and me on our own, with four dogs who are as scared as we are.

Every other time I've wanted to find a home for one of the rescued dogs, I've been able to reach inside and bring out "friendly Wes." That's what Kat calls me when I kick into gear to gain the confidence of strangers so they'll trust me to give them a good pet.

The first time Kat saw friendly Wes, I was placing an Irish setter with the perfect owners, an older woman and her teenage grandson. Kat waited until they left with their new dog. Then she stomped up behind me and demanded to know who I was and what I'd done with the real Wes.

Now, standing outside Nice Manor, I'm wondering what I've done with friendly Wes. I could use him about now because I'm feeling more like Mad Dog with every minute. Mrs. Coolidge should have given us more time to work with the dogs. She should have set everything up for us at the Manor. She shouldn't have left us to face them alone.

"You okay?" Dakota asks. She's staring at me, probably wishing Eddy Barker were standing here instead of Wes "Mad Dog" Williams.

"Okay?" I ask, the sarcasm not coming from friendly Wes. "What's not to be okay about, Dakota? Let's go meet old people." I lead the way through the covered porch and into Nice Manor.

I was wrong about the place only looking good on the outside. If anything, Nice Manor is even nicer on the inside. The entryway is all wood and plush carpet, with a fireplace and sofas. I can see past it to a dining room with white tablecloths and flowers. Glassed-in shelves run the length of the hallway, filled with fancy plates and little glass animals. My grandma would have loved this stuff. Come to think of it, this place smells a lot like my grandmother's apartment did.

"*Pssst!* This way!"

I pivot in the direction of the whisper, but I don't see anybody. Not until I look down.

A woman rolls her wheelchair into the hall, then back, disappearing through a dark doorway.

"What was that?" Dakota whispers.

I shrug. The bulldog growls.

A hand appears through the doorway, a lone finger crooked and motioning us into the dark room.

I glance at Dakota. She stays where she is, the Blab's leash in one hand, the terrier's in the other.

"Well?" comes a scratchy voice. "Don't just stand there. Get in here!"

Dakota and I herd the dogs into the room. The second we're in, the old woman wheels over and rams her wheelchair into the door, forcing it shut. A T-shirt has been duct-taped to the door, covering the window and blocking all views from the hall.

"Lights, girlie." The woman points to a switch too high for her to reach from her wheelchair.

"Sorry," Dakota says, scurrying to turn on the light.

"Why?" the woman demands. "Are you the one who put that switch up so high?"

The overhead light gives me my first good look at the woman in the wheelchair. She's short and wide. Her body overflows the wheelchair seat. Wisps of gray hair spring out from under her Chicago Cubs cap, which is on sideways. Spindly legs stick out from a gray skirt. She's wearing a Chicago White Sox sweatshirt and high-top tennis shoes. Her face and neck aren't so much wrinkled as they are baggy, like maybe a long time ago her face was twice this big, and when it shrank, her skin didn't.

"Buddy?" Dakota asks.

The woman's pudgy face lights up. "So my reputation precedes me." She winks at us. "How is the old Coolidge busybody these days?"

"She's okay," Dakota answers. "I guess."

Buddy eyes Dakota, then me, then the dogs scrambling at our feet, trying to get out of here. "Are you fans?" she asks, looking skeptical.

"I like baseball," Dakota volunteers.

"But who do you root for?" Buddy demands.

Dakota grins. "The underdog."

Buddy breaks into a gap-toothed smile, until she turns to me. "How about you? We have to get these important matters settled first. Cubs? White Sox? Which is it?"

She's making me nervous. "Both," I answer. "Especially the Sox."

Buddy claps her hands, sending the terrier to hide behind Dakota. "All right, then! Let's roll!" She puts two fingers to her lips and lets out a piercing whistle.

A closet door flings open in the back of the room. People hobble out. It's a parade of old people. Two are pushing walkers as they all shuffle to a row of folding chairs.

Buddy whistles again. The bulldog jerks away, yanking the leash out of my hands.

"Come back here!" I call. But I haven't worked on the "come" command.

The dog dashes toward Buddy and slides halfway across the freckled linoleum floor, not stopping until she slams into Buddy's wheelchair.

"Sorry!" I run up and grab the bulldog's leash. "I haven't trained the dogs yet."

"Obviously," Buddy observes.

"This wouldn't have happened if I'd had more time to work with them." I can see the whole project slipping away, the dogs going back to the pound.

Suddenly, the bulldog lunges at the wheelchair and jumps up, planting her front paws on Buddy's knees.

"No!" I cry.

Buddy waves me off. "I reckon this one likes me." She scratches the ugly dog on her chest.

I let out a breath I didn't realize I was holding. "I think you're right." Maybe Buddy and the rest of them will give our dogs a chance after all.

Buddy stares into the bulldog's face. The dog stares back. Their heads are inches apart. It's eerie how much they look alike with saggy faces, pug noses, and deep brown eyes.

"Ugly ol' girl, isn't she?" Buddy comments.

As if in reply, the dog's mouth opens in a big smile.

Dakota gasps.

Someone behind me says, "EEEeeeyew!"

And out of the dog's mouth comes a giant glob of slobber—right onto Buddy's lap.

THIRTEEN

"GROSS!"

"Oh my."

"Now that's what I call disgusting."

The old folks circle Buddy and the bulldog.

I tug at the dog's collar, but she doesn't want to leave her new friend.

Dakota rushes off somewhere and comes back with a handful of paper towels. I have no idea where she found them. She wipes up the ball of slobber from Buddy's lap and drops the towels into the wastebasket.

I'm not sure what to do now. Buddy was

our inside man, the one person Mrs. Coolidge said was on our side. Now we've probably lost her.

"I'm really sorry, ma'am," I say, reaching for friendly Wes. I yank the dog away from her, but she pops back up. "The dog's never acted like this before. If you'll give me a chance, I can train her not to—"

Buddy holds up her hand for me to stop. She frowns and moves her face closer to the bulldog's. "This mutt reminds me of a fella I used to know. Pitched for the Giants. Chewed tobacco. Ugly habit, chewing that stuff. Bad for the breath too."

Nobody argues.

"Well, what are you all standing around me for?" Buddy demands. "Sit down."

I get the bulldog back under control while Dakota helps the old people to their seats. There are six of them, counting Buddy.

I hand the bulldog's leash to Dakota so she has three leashes. I'm only holding the Pomeranian. When I face our audience, I'm not sure what to say. One-on-one I'm okay with wannabe pet owners, but this is different.

Buddy breaks the silence. "Go! Go!

Whaddya say? Give us all a show today! Go! Go! Whaddya say? Give us all a show today! Go, fight, win!" From under her wheelchair, she pulls out two blue and white pom-poms and waves them above her head. "Go, dogs!"

A few of the others join in clapping or venturing a weak "hurray" or "yea."

Dakota comes up next to me and takes the Pom from my hands. "Wes, what do we do now?"

I swallow hard and let a prayer slip out from somewhere inside me, a place I don't seem to have control over. When I tell Popeye I don't pray, he usually smiles and says, "Sure you do, Wes." And I guess he's right. I don't pray like he does. Or Annie, or Kat. Or even Dakota lately. I don't know how. Still, it's like something inside of me knows more than I do about praying. And I know enough to admit I could use all the help I can get about now.

"Thanks for coming," I begin, relaxing a little. Maybe that prayer is working. "I'm Wes Williams. I've already met the charming Miss Buddy, and I intend to get to know the rest of you. But first, I'd like you to meet your new best friends: a three-legged Pomeranian, an extremely shy terrier mix, a beagle-Lab mix, a bulldog mix, and Dakota Brown. I'll let you guess which one is Dakota."

I get the laughs I deserve, along with an elbow in my chest from Dakota, which I guess I deserve too. But she's grinning and whispers, "Way to go, Wes."

The old folks introduce themselves. To remember their names I use association, the memory trick my grandma taught me not long before she died. Rose has pink cheeks and is frail as a rose. April and June are sitting together, and I try to picture April's long, stringy hair out in April showers and June's round nose with a fat june bug on it. Sitting as far away from the dogs as possible is Velva, dressed up like she's headed to church. So I picture Velva in velvet on a velvet church pew.

There's only one man in the group. He's kind of short and skinny as a dog's tail.

"My name is Leon," he says. I'm trying to come up with a way to remember his name when he adds, "If you forget my name, think of Christmas, the first Noel! Leon is *Noel* backwards."

"Cool. Thanks, guys." I walk down the

row of spectators and repeat their names, getting them all right. "Names are important. Your dogs know that. That's why we haven't named these dogs yet."

"They don't got names?" Buddy says. "Boo!" She turns to the others. "Give 'em the Bronx cheer for that one," she urges.

A few of her friends join her in booing me for not naming the dogs.

"Take it easy," I plead. "I couldn't name the dogs. Not without you guys. An important part of the basic training for these dogs is language. They're going to learn your language, including what you call them. In fact, a dog's name is the most important word you'll teach him. Now do you see why I couldn't name the dogs without you?"

"Let's call this one Buddy," Leon suggests, pointing to the ugly bulldog.

Buddy leans forward in her wheelchair and throws a paper wad at Leon. "Strike one for you, *Noel*!" she hollers. "Maybe we ought to name this scared terrier here Noel."

I figure I better break this up before they really go at each other. "Hold on a minute, okay? Before we name the dogs, before we teach the dogs *our* language, we need to learn theirs."

While I've been working the people crowd, Dakota's been working the dogs. She's managed to get all four dogs to either lie down or sit close to her.

"Take a look at these dogs." I point to them, and everybody gets quiet. "They're talking to us right now," I explain. "Can you tell what they're saying?"

Nobody answers. Rose taps her hearing aid, as if that's the problem.

I kneel next to the Blab. "See this guy's ears? They're pricked up toward us. He's asking, 'What do you want?'" I stroke the Blab's chest. "Look at this mouth. He's got a lopsided grin that's saying, 'Hey! Come closer, will you?' And this tail, straight up like that, says, 'I'm paying attention. I'm not going to miss a trick, man.'"

I move to the terrier, who's lying on the floor, ears back, tail clamped. "These ears are begging me not to hurt her. She's saying, 'I'm sorry. Don't punish me.'"

Several *aw*s travel the row of spectators.

"I would never punish this dog, but

somebody has," I explain. "We need to learn her language and help her learn ours so she won't be afraid of us any longer." When I stroke the terrier's side, she rolls over on her back. "Now she's saying, '*Please* don't hurt me. I give.'" I scratch her stomach and move to the next dog.

"I think this beautiful girl is a cross between a boxer and a bulldog," I say.

"Buddy all over again!" Leon shouts.

Buddy shouts back, "Strike two, Noel."

I laugh. "These big eyes, wide open like this, are saying, 'Just so you know, I'm the boss around here.' I've never seen this dog pull her lips back and show her teeth. But if she does, I'll be careful because she'll be telling me, 'Watch out! I don't want you around here.'"

"What about the poor little crippled dog?" Velva asks. She puts one hand on her walker, as if letting me know she understands the Pomeranian's problem. "What's that little dog trying to tell us?"

I get down on all fours until I'm eye-to-eye with the Pomeranian. He hops around, then gives me a soft-eyed sideways glance.

"There," I say. "Did you hear that?"

"I didn't hear anything," Buddy answers.

Rose taps her hearing aid again.

"That sideways glance," I explain. "He's saying, 'Wes, you're cool. You know that?'"

They laugh.

I'm still on my hands and knees, so I smile up at the audience. The Pom moves in and licks my face as I'm getting to my feet.

"Excuse me?" June asks, raising her hand like she's in elementary school. "I've always wanted to know something. When a dog licks your face, is it akin to a kiss?"

I don't answer right away because it's not an easy question. I've always thought that when a dog licked me, it was kind of a thank-you. Like, "Thanks for making me happy." But I'm not sure what people's kisses mean. No experience there.

Dakota speaks up. "I heard that hungry pups in the wild lick their mothers' and fathers' mouths. Usually they do that because the adult dogs eat first, chew the food, and then let their kids lick the mushy, chewed-up food gunk from their mouths. Sounds pretty gross, but it works. When the food's gone, most pups still lick their parents' mouths, kind of like a thank-you kiss. So I vote yes. A lick is a kiss."

"The lady is as smart as she is beautiful!" Leon exclaims.

It's a great answer, and I'm guessing she got it from Barker.

That question leads to more questions about dogs.

June raises her hand again, and I nod for her to go ahead. "Why do dogs wag their tails?"

I motion for Dakota to take over.

"Well," she begins, "I think it could mean one of two things: 'Great to see you, June,' or 'Hey, June, you wanna fight?'"

Dakota gets some decent laughs on that one, then goes on to explain what to look for when a dog's tail is wagging. "If the tail is straight and stiff, like a metronome or a pendulum, you might be in for trouble. Otherwise, if it's a fast, loose wag, think of it as a friendly wave."

"Look at that little three-legged sweetheart," April says. "Is he crying?"

The dog is whimpering, and it does kinda sound like a cry. I pick him up and search for a favorite spot he likes scratched. I think I find it on his left side, but he's still stiff and wary.

"Dogs don't cry with tears," Dakota

explains, reaching over to stroke the Pom too. "But they do cry. Look at his tail. It's down, and his head is hanging low like that."

We're quiet for a second, and I think we're all rooting for the Pom.

Then Buddy bellows out, "Now why do they do that?" She points to the bulldog, who's scratching up a storm.

"Ah," Dakota says, sounding mysterious and wise, "now that's one of deepest, darkest secrets of a dog whisperer." She glances around the room. Every eye is on her. The crowd grows totally quiet, waiting for her answer. "Dogs scratch–" she pauses dramatically–"because they have an itch."

Buddy bursts out laughing.

When the laughter dies down, I forge ahead. "Okay. Now it's time to teach the dogs a little people language. As promised, we're going to start with the most important word of all, the name."

Before I can stop them, everybody's shouting out names.

"I had a Pomeranian just like that one when I was a girl," Rose says, her voice dreamy. "We should call him Pom-Pom."

"What kind of name is that for a boy dog?" Buddy demands. "Let's call him 'the Babe' or 'Shoeless Joe.'" She wheels her chair out of line. "I got it. Tinker. Who remembers the famous Cubs slogan: 'Tinker to Evers to Chance'?"

"Wait a minute!" I wave my arms like a major league ump until Buddy settles down again. "Let me tell you what goes into a good name besides baseball history, okay? First, choose a short name that won't be shortened. If you end up calling the dog Westmoreland and Westie and West, the poor dog won't know what his real name is."

"I never thought of that," Dakota admits. "Makes sense. What else?"

"Use the name once you've given it to your dog. Don't call him Baby or Sweetie Pie or Puppy Wuppy."

Dakota grins. "Only if you promise to say Puppy Wuppy again."

I keep going. "Always say the dog's name first, before the command. Like, 'Moxie, here!'"

The crouching terrier perks up, gets to her feet, and walks over to me.

"Looks like that one's got a name," April

comments. "I like that name. Moxie. Nice ring to it, don't you think, June?"

I don't think I've ever heard the name before, and I have no idea where it came from. I pet the terrier. "Moxie," I tell her, "if that's the name you want, that's the name you'll get. And nobody here will call you Mox or Moxerama or the Moxster, right?"

Without too many arguments, we finally agree on names for all four dogs:

Moxie, the terrier

Lion, the three-legged Pomeranian

Bag, the beagle-Lab mix, so Buddy can make her "doggie Bag" jokes

Munch, the bulldog, also thanks to Buddy

We practice calling the dogs by their new names. Then I start to wind us down. "Thanks, everybody. You've been great."

"Nope," Buddy says. "*You've* been great." She turns to her friends. "Right, fans? Let's do it!" She raises her arms, then lowers them.

The others fall in and move their arms like Buddy. They look like geese after a really hard winter.

"Wes," Dakota whispers, laughing and

leaning into me, "don't you get it? They're doing the wave."

I watch for a full minute while Buddy leads the "crowd" in the oldest wave in the history of the world.

When the waves finally die down, I thank them again. Then I turn to the dogs and thank them, too. "If we can learn dog language the way these dogs are starting to learn ours, we'll have it made."

"Are you kidding?" Buddy asks. "Why, we know their language. *Arf!*" She barks again. "*Arf! Arf!*"

June barks next. April joins in with several small-dog yaps. Even Rose and Velva get in the act.

Leon lets loose with an all-out wolf howl: "*Ah-ah-oooo! Ah-ah-oooo!*"

They're barking and howling. The dogs get caught up in the commotion. Munch and Bag bark and yap at the old folks. It's about the funniest thing I've ever seen.

The door bursts open. In walks a woman who looks about Mrs. Coolidge's age, only bouncy. If she were one of the dogs, she'd be Bag, the hyper beagle-Lab.

"Stop this riot at once!" she screams. She turns to Dakota and me. "What do you people think you're doing here?"

"I . . . we . . ." I can't get words out fast enough.

The bulldog charges the door and jumps on the woman, knocking her back a step. She shoves the dog with one hand and points to the door with the other. "Get out of here right this minute, or I'm calling the cops!"

FOURTEEN

DAKOTA AND I ARE USHERED OUT of the room, along with all the dogs. We're both sputtering explanations and excuses.

"We weren't hurting anybody," Dakota mutters.

"We're supposed to be here to—" I try.

"Not today, you weren't. Now shoo!" The woman acts like she's shooing flies from a picnic.

"Mrs. Coolidge sent us," Dakota says.

The woman stops in the entryway. Maybe Dakota's said the magic words: *Mrs. Coolidge.*

"Mrs. Coolidge sent you?" the woman repeats. "She did, did she?"

We nod. But I'm not feeling the magic.

"Well, you can tell Georgette Coolidge for me that she's way out of line this time. She's gone too far. That woman is going to get all of us shut down by the state boards. Is that what she wants?"

Dakota tries to answer. "I'm sure she didn't mean to–"

"*I'm* the one who has to talk to the licensing board," the woman says. "And who has to face state officials who don't approve of pets in assisted-living facilities? Not Georgette Coolidge. *Me.* Poor Miss Golf, the lowly activities director."

I was pretty sure that's who she was. Whatever history she and Mrs. Coolidge have can't have been good.

"Didn't you agree to try Mrs. Coolidge's pilot pet project?" Dakota insists. "Mrs. Coolidge said the Manor was behind it. Our job was just to get dogs for the residents. So we–"

"*Dog!* Not *dogs!*" Miss Golf interrupts. "Georgette and I have been all through this. I said I'd try out *a dog.* Who do you think's going to end up taking care of a pet around here? Anybody else look ready to walk a dog come winter?"

"But I can train the dogs to—"

She won't let me finish. "*Dog!* And now that I've seen you people in action, I don't think even one dog will work out. I've got enough to do without all this bother and noise. No. I'm sorry. This isn't going to work. I'm sure you meant well."

"Wait," Dakota pleads. "You can't quit without giving us a chance."

Miss Golf leads us to the entryway. "Tell Mrs. Coolidge I'm sorry things didn't work out."

Dakota picks up the terrier. That's when I see it. The dog's so scared she's left a puddle in the entrance.

The director stares down at the dog puddle as if it's toxic. "That's just great. Do you have any idea what the state would do if the inspector walked in right now?"

"I'll clean it up," I offer.

"Never mind," she says. "Good-bye. And you can tell Georgette Coolidge that she needs to learn to go through proper channels." She shuts the door, leaving Dakota and me and our dogs outside.

Dakota sighs. "Well, that went well, wouldn't you say?" She digs into her pocket for her cell. "I'll call Mrs. C. to come get us."

I feel stupid standing on the front step, so I walk Munch and Bag up the sidewalk.

From behind a tree comes a flash of sunlight. It takes me a second to realize the sun's reflecting off a silver wheelchair. Buddy rolls out in front of me. "You left without saying good-bye."

"Yeah, well . . ." What does she expect? "Anyway, I'm really sorry things didn't work out." But mostly, I'm sorry for the dogs. It's not going to be easy finding homes for these dogs.

"Don't be daft," Buddy says. "Didn't you ever hear of a comeback?" She tips her ball cap and wheels her chair toward the Manor again. "See you Friday!"

I shout after her, "They told us we can't come back."

"Bosh!" Buddy shouts, not looking back at us. "Leave everything to Buddy. See you on Friday!"

∗ ∗ ∗

Inside Mrs. Coolidge's sedan, Dakota and I take turns filling Mrs. Coolidge in on our failure. We have to shout because the dogs won't stop barking.

"That woman, Miss Golf, threatened to call the cops," I tell her.

"Buddy is so cool, though," Dakota says. "She followed us outside and told us she'd see us on Friday. I'd like to go back and visit all of them. But I don't see how we can go there again, with or without the dogs."

"No kidding," I mutter.

"Nonsense," Mrs. Coolidge argues. "If Buddy says to go back on Friday, we go back on Friday."

"But what about the activities lady? She said she'd call the police." No way I'm getting into trouble with the police just when my mom's getting out of it.

"Mercy," Mrs. Coolidge says. "Carolyn Golf is no match for Buddy." She turns onto the country road that takes us to the farm. "Didn't Miss Golf send a message for me?"

Dakota and I exchange glances. I'm

not about to deliver the activities director's messages.

"Well?" Mrs. Coolidge demands.

I wait it out, and Dakota breaks. "She did send a couple of messages," she admits. When Mrs. Coolidge drums the steering wheel and sighs, Dakota tells her about "dog" instead of "dogs" and about the state inspectors checking up. She leaves out the part about going through proper channels.

"Why don't we go back Saturday?" Mrs. Coolidge suggests. "I think that's Carol's day off."

"I can't go Saturday," I say quickly.

"Wes is going to Chicago to see his mom," Dakota explains.

"Ah." Mrs. Coolidge glances at me, but she doesn't ask. "Friday it is then. I'll pick you up first thing." She almost misses the turn into the drive. She swerves left, then right. The dogs start barking.

"Look!" Dakota shouts over the loud barking. "Somebody's here."

A small red car is parked crooked by the house. I recognize it. "It's Ms. Bean."

"The social worker?" Mrs. Coolidge asks.

"What's she doing here?" Dakota demands.

I get a weird chill, like something electric running through me. "Probably checking up on you, Dakota."

"Me?"

"Yeah, you. Popeye and Annie are sending you back. Didn't they tell you?"

Dakota punches me, and Mrs. Coolidge chuckles.

But the chill inside of me doesn't go away.

Mrs. Coolidge pulls up her sedan behind Ms. Bean's beater. The car's empty except for the usual water bottles, food wrappers, and notebooks.

Popeye comes out of the house with Ms. Bean. I start unloading the dogs. I snap on leashes and open kennels, all without looking up.

Behind me, Mrs. Coolidge and Dakota exchange greetings with Ms. Bean. Still, I won't look at them. If I don't look, then she won't talk to me. She won't have news—bad news—for me.

Ms. Bean says something too soft for me to hear. The others grow quiet. I lift the Pom, Lion, out of the car. I don't want to let him go, even though he's squirming to get down with the others.

Footsteps—Ms. Bean's footsteps—come closer. "Wes?"

My throat feels like something's stuck in it, which must be why my words come out thin and broken. "Hey . . . Ms. . . . . Bean."

"Could I talk to you a minute, Wes?" she asks.

I shrug. "I'm kinda busy."

Dakota appears and reaches for Lion. I don't want to hand him over, but I do. Dakota's biting her bottom lip, and her eyes look wet. Maybe *she's* the one Ms. Bean's here for, after all.

"I'll walk the dogs," Dakota says. "No sweat." She scoops up Lion and whisks away the other dogs.

"Thanks, Dakota," Popeye says. He steps toward me and Ms. Bean. "Wes, Ms. Bean needs to talk with you about your mother. Do you want me to leave you two alone?"

I shake my head hard. I'm not sure why, but I don't want him to leave. I want *her* to leave. I want Ms. Bean to go back to Chicago, to take her news with her, to talk about anything except my mother.

Popeye leads us back to the house. Out of the corner of my eye, I see Hank jogging from the barn to help Dakota with the dogs. Rex trots out with Hank, sees me, and comes racing, tail wagging. He doesn't stop until he's beside me. His head slides under my hand for an automatic pat.

We go inside and settle at the table, with Ms. Bean on the end and Popeye across from me. Rex lies down by my chair.

"What?" It's the only word I can get out. My head is trying to move past the blockades I've set there, the things I never want to think about. The possibilities. This is about my mother, and it isn't good.

"Wes," Ms. Bean says, sneaking a glance at Popeye first, "your mother signed herself out of rehab yesterday."

I wait. Is that it? "So what?" I ask, relief spreading like melted snow in my chest. "She's getting out on Saturday anyway. What's the big deal?"

"Part of her agreement with the county

court was that she'd stay in rehab," Ms. Bean says. "She broke that agreement."

"She was in that place almost 90 days!" I shout. Rex starts barking. I pet him, but he won't stop. "So she left a few days early? Maybe she wanted to start looking for a place to live." I wish she'd called me, though. She should have called. I could have come up early. I could have helped. "Why are they making such a big deal out of this?" I demand.

"Take it easy, Wes," Popeye says. "Ms. Bean isn't the problem here."

But my heart is beating too hard to stop my words. "This isn't fair! Why don't they leave her alone?"

"There's another problem," Ms. Bean continues. "A bigger problem. The police picked her up today—"

"No way!" I get to my feet. My chair scoots back, ramming into Rex. But I can't help it. "The cops have it in for her! What do they want? How do they expect her to make a fresh start? Or *us* to make a fresh start?"

Popeye motions for me to sit down. "Wes, you have to listen. Your mother was picked up for using again. They found drugs on her. She was in pretty bad shape."

I sit, but my head is still spinning. This can't be happening. She promised. She promised she wouldn't do this again. "There's some mistake. You'll see. I need to talk to her. I want to hear what *she* says. I don't believe you. I don't believe any of this."

Ms. Bean folds her hands on the table. Her hands are smooth, with long fingernails painted pink. Not like my mother's hands. My mother's hands never looked like that. "I'm pretty sure they're going to send her back to rehab. That's good. This is her third offense. Things could be a lot worse for her."

I don't want to hear how much worse things could be. "Where is she now?" Rex starts barking again. Or maybe he's been barking the whole time, and now he's turning up the volume. I don't know which. "Is she okay?"

I catch the look Ms. Bean exchanges with Popeye, a flash of eyes filled with sympathy and pity. I hate that look.

"Where is she?" I demand.

"Your mother is being held in county," Ms. Bean explains. "She'll be there over the weekend.

147

But I'm working with her public defender to get her back into rehab as soon as possible."

Ms. Bean doesn't say the word *jail*. Nobody uses that word around me. But that's what it is.

"Wes?" She moves closer. "Did you hear me? I'm hoping to get your mother back into rehab in a few days. As soon as she's settled in again, I'll arrange for another visit."

My head snaps up. "I don't want another visit. I'm visiting my mom on Saturday. *This* Saturday."

"I don't think that's such a good idea," Ms. Bean says.

But she's wrong. She's wrong about everything. And she's dead wrong about this. "I get to see my mom on Saturday. You said you'd take me. You promised!" I shout. I have to because Rex is barking so loud I can't hear myself think.

"Please try to understand," Ms. Bean pleads. She looks so sad, so flustered, that I could almost feel sorry for her. But I *don't* feel sorry for her. I don't have enough "sorry" left for her.

"I understand, all right." My fingernails dig

148

into my palms. But my nails are as short as Ms. Bean's are long, and even that makes me mad.

"Wes, I'm sorry. The plan was for me to drive you to the rehab facility for an arranged visit. That's no longer possible."

This time I jump up from the table so fast my chair crashes to the floor. Rex scurries out of the way. The barking stops. "My mom is expecting me to come! I'm not going to let her down. I'm going to see her!" I shout. I picture Mom, crossing off calendar days like I have been. She almost made it. Almost. She really tried. I know she tried. And I'm not going to punish her like everybody else. I'm not breaking my promise.

"Wes," Ms. Bean says, trying to reason with me, "this is county lockup we're talking about. Wouldn't it be better for you to wait until she's back in rehab and you can sit next to her instead of looking through glass and talking on a two-way phone?"

What does she know about what's better for me?

My chest is heaving. I feel like I could throw up. "I'm seeing my mom on Saturday if I have to walk to Chicago."

FIFTEEN

As soon as we get rid of Ms. Bean, Popeye tries to calm me down. Finally, he volunteers to drive me to Chicago himself on Saturday. I'm holding him to it.

I stay in my room the rest of the night and let Dakota and Hank take over with the dogs and Blackfire. I want to do it myself, to take care of the dogs. But I don't even feel like climbing down the stairs when dinner rolls around. Annie brings me a plate of fried chicken, and Kat comes up later with a brownie. I can't eat any of it.

I have no clue how long I've been sitting

in the dark when Kat knocks on the door again. "Want me to walk Rex for you?"

I'm sitting on the floor. Rex is stretched out beside me, his head on my knee. I'm not sure, but I guess he's been with me the whole time. "Yeah. Thanks, Kat."

"Come on, Rex," she calls from the doorway.

Rex doesn't budge.

"Go on. Go for a walk," I tell him. He doesn't move, so I raise my voice. "Go!"

Still, he doesn't move. His head stays stretched over my leg.

"I mean it, Rex." My head is electric, buzzing like bad phone lines. "Get!" I shake my leg and make his head drop off me.

"Wes, don't." Kat walks over and takes Rex by the collar. "Come on, Rex. Come with me." Still, she has to half drag him out.

I get up and slam the door behind them.

✵ ✵ ✵

Thursday moves along without any help from Wes "Mad Dog" Williams. I can't get my mom out of my head. I want it to be Saturday. I want to see her. Everything will be okay when I see her. I picture her thinking about me, thinking the same thing I am—that if she just sees me, things will be okay. We can still go ahead with our plans.

Once, when we lived above the bar, Mom came home late, crying. Her hair was wild, and she had a black eye. I tried everything I could think of to get her to stop crying. I stood on my head, sang a song she liked. I colored her a picture and glued bottle caps to it. It was summer, but I made her a valentine. Finally, she stopped crying and hugged me. "You're the only one, Wesley," she told me. "You're the only one who can make me stop crying like a baby."

I wonder if she remembers that. I hope she does.

✷ ✷ ✷

"Wes, telephone!" Dakota knocks on my door and hollers again. "Phone, Wes! For you."

I roll over and check the clock on my bedside table. It's after 10. I haven't slept this late since I came to Starlight Animal Rescue. No one has. "Go away." I pull the pillow over my head.

She knocks again. "It's Mrs. Coolidge, and she won't take no for an answer."

I drag myself out of bed and step on Rex. He jumps up, then sits again, eyes fixed on me. I hope somebody walked him already. I stumble to the door and open it. "Tell her I'm sick."

Mrs. Coolidge's voice shoots from the phone in Dakota's hands. Even that far away, she's loud and clear. "Bosh! Get on this phone this instant, Wesley!"

Dakota shoves the receiver into my hand. I lift it to my ear. I know what Mrs. Coolidge wants. It's Friday. We're supposed to go back to Nice Manor and train the dogs. "Mrs. Coolidge," I begin, "I don't feel like—"

"Feel schmeel, banana peel," she says. "I'll be by for you and Dakota and all four dogs in one hour. Do *not* keep me waiting." Mrs. Coolidge hangs up.

Dakota takes the phone I hold out. She doesn't ask, but she's obviously waiting for an answer.

At her feet, the three-legged Lion is play-fighting with the terrier, Moxie. I started this. I have to finish it, no matter how I "feel schmeel." "Okay," I say, giving in.

"Cool!" Dakota picks up both dogs. "I'll get the dogs ready if you'll get *you* ready."

"What?"

"Let's just say that compared to you, Munch smells like roses."

I look down, surprised to see that I haven't changed my clothes in two days.

✳ ✳ ✳

Things are so rushed trying to get the dogs ready for this that I don't get a chance to really talk to Dakota until we're standing out front, waiting for Mrs. Coolidge. "Thanks for taking the dogs for me the last couple of days," I say, not looking at her.

"Hank helped," Dakota says. "These guys are growing on me. They're good dogs, aren't they?"

I nod. "All dogs are good dogs until people mess them up. How's Blackfire? Sorry I dropped the ball on that deal."

Her grin dissolves. "Well, lucky for you, you'll still get your chance to help with him. He's not any better."

"You're kidding."

She shakes her head. "Hank says there's no infection. But that abscess hasn't drained at all. It's still festering in his hoof. I want it to come out so he can start to heal."

Something inside of me knots up. *Festering*. It's a word I've never used, but I think I know what it feels like.

As if Dakota can read my mind, she says, "Wes, I wish I could help. Like, I wish I knew a Bible verse to give you for your mom and stuff. Kat could."

"That's okay." I know Kat's verses have helped Dakota since she's been here. Dakota never talks about running away anymore, and she's . . . I don't know, more peaceful. But that stuff doesn't work on me. "I'll be okay when I see my mom."

She nods, and we wait in silence until Mrs. Coolidge drives up.

Dakota and Mrs. Coolidge talk on the way to Nice Manor, but I tune them out. My mind is locked on my mom. I imagine her sitting in jail, counting down the hours until my visit.

When we pull up to the Manor, Buddy and her archrival, Miss Golf, the activities director, come out to meet us. The two women look like opposing coaches who've agreed to put on a united front for the sake of the game. Buddy's wearing what looks like an official Chicago Bears jersey with her Cubs ball cap. Miss Golf, in a pink jogging suit, reminds me of a pink lemonade Popsicle, like my grandma used to make in her freezer.

"How are you, Carol?" Mrs. Coolidge hollers out the window. "You're looking in the pink today." She doesn't make a move to get out of the car. Instead, she revs the engine, making Dakota and me move faster to get the dogs out.

"I'm just fine, Georgette. And you?" Miss Golf returns, the frost in her voice fitting right in with the Popsicle image. "Let's get this straight from the get-go: Nice Manor will consider adopting one dog. *One.* I'm allowing you to bring four so that we can choose one. That is, *if* any of the dogs work out, which at this point seems like a long shot."

Finally, I get the last dog out of the car.

"Nonsense," Mrs. Coolidge mutters. Then before Miss Golf has a chance to react, Mrs. Coolidge shouts, "Have fun!" and drives off waving.

157

Buddy wheels closer. She lifts the cowering terrier onto her lap. "I told Miss Golf she was welcome to spy on our clandestine canine activities today," she says.

"I'm not spying," Miss Golf protests. "It's my responsibility to make sure nothing threatens the—"

"Time out!" Buddy signals, making the classic T with her bony hands. "Let's kick off this game. Play ball!"

I reach for Moxie, thinking the terrier will be scared with Buddy yelling like an out-of-control ref. But Moxie's ears perk up, and she tries to lick the old woman's face.

"You bet, Moxie!" Buddy hollers. "Let's show 'em what we're made of!"

The others are waiting for us in the rec room, the same place we brought the dogs Wednesday. They shout greetings as we walk in. Munch, Bag, and even little Lion wag their tails and scurry around, greeting their new pack.

Dakota and I stand up in front. I know everybody's waiting for me to get things started, but I can't wrap my mind around what we're even doing here. It's like I'm already on my way to Chicago to see Mom.

After a couple of minutes of strained silence, Dakota takes over. "Great to see you guys again." Her voice is shaky, but she keeps going. I don't try to stop her. "Okay," Dakota continues, "where do you think we parked this morning?" She doesn't wait for the answer. I know the answer. Popeye has told this one a million times. "In the *barking* lot!" Dakota finishes.

Leon hoots, and Buddy whistles through her teeth.

I get them to sit in twos. April and June. Velva and Rose. Leon and Buddy. "We're going to work in pairs to get the dogs used to things. Usually a dog's socialization time comes in the first three or four months of life, but with these guys we need to start over."

I dole out the dogs, giving Lion to Velva and Rose, and Bag the Blab to April and June. The terrier, Moxie, is still on Buddy's lap, so that one stays with Buddy and Leon.

That leaves the slobbering Munch, who's about twice as big as the other dogs. There's only one solution. "Miss Golf, you and Dakota will need to team up for Munch."

"Munch?" she repeats.

I scratch Munch's ears. "This cute little girl."

Miss Golf's eyes grow to golf ball–size. "I'm just an observer. Besides, isn't this the one that spits?"

Dakota takes Munch's leash and slides onto the seat next to Miss Golf. "Munch is a sweetie," she promises. "You'll see."

"I'm not good with pets," Velva says, scooting her chair farther away from Rose, her partner. "What if I hurt this poor little one's leg?"

"Too late for that," Rose replies. She hugs the Pom, and the wrecked leg sways, as if Lion is waving at Velva.

I get them to do the basic bonding exercises, stroking the dogs' backs, then their heads, then the ears. "Don't forget the inside of the ears. Some dogs will do anything for you if they think it will get them a good ear scratching. Same goes for a tummy rub. Whenever you can, get yourself low with your dog. If you're eye level with a dog, it says that you're not trying to hurt him or take over his turf."

Leon gets down on the ground to look into Moxie's eyes. The terrier wags her tail. "She likes me!" Leon declares. "Just like every woman."

"Foul! Out of bounds," Buddy cries.

I want to get caught up in the bonding too. But it feels like I'm watching all of this from the moon. When I tune back in to the voices in the room, I hear April's baby talk: "That's a good little Baggie. Ooh, my Bagger Wagger."

I've already told them about sticking to one form of the dog's name.

Then I hear Dakota: "Munchie, you sweetheart. What a nice Munchster you are! How's my Baroness von Munchster?"

"Dakota!" I shout. She should know better than that. "What's the matter with you? Are you crazy?"

The room goes silent. Everyone stares at me.

"What did I do?" Dakota asks.

I hadn't meant to shout that loud. I take a deep breath and hold in the fury that feels like it could explode. "Don't forget to call the dogs only by their real names, okay?"

"Oops," she says, turning back to Munch. "Forgot about that one, didn't I, Munchie—I mean, Munch."

I let them go back to the bonding exercises while I pace the room. When I turn around,

I almost trip over Buddy's wheelchair. She's rolled into my pacing lane. "Is there a problem with Moxie?" I ask her.

She shakes her head. "Is there a problem with you?"

I fake a smile. "'Course not."

"Sure you don't want to call it a day? I can round up the team and get them back tomorrow, if you want," she offers.

"I won't be here tomorrow." The answer is too loud, as if she's just threatened to *make* me be here tomorrow. I lower my voice and explain. "I'm visiting my mom tomorrow. In Chicago."

"That right?" she asks.

I nod. "I haven't seen her for a long time."

"Her move or yours?" Buddy asks.

"Not mine," I answer quickly.

"That what's got you angry as a sacked quarterback on a muddy field?"

The question throws me. "I'm not angry. Not at my mom."

"Right," Buddy says. "Well then, you tell her for me that she's got one fine son."

Before I can thank her—or argue with

162

her—she wheels back to Leon and the terrier, who are nose-to-nose on the floor.

I finish the session early and get Dakota to call Mrs. Coolidge to pick us up. Then I try to figure out how I'll get through the rest of the hours before I'm face-to-face with my mother.

SIXTEEN

SATURDAY MORNING I'm ready two hours before Popeye's takeoff time. I don't know if I slept at all. My thoughts kept bumping into each other. I tried to imagine what I'd say to Mom, what she'd say to me, how she'd look. I pictured her lying awake too, worrying about what we'll talk about.

Hank tears into the house with Dakota on his heels.

"Hank! Answer me!" she shouts. For the last few days, Hank has been Dakota's horse helper instead of me.

"Dakota, we're doing everything we can," he says.

"Then why isn't Blackfire better? Why isn't the sore draining? Maybe nothing's there?"

"The abscess is there, Dakota." Hank sounds more frustrated than I got with her. "I guarantee pus and junk are inside that hoof."

"You don't know that," Dakota snaps.

Hank stops and looks down on Dakota. He's over six feet tall, but he's still no match for her. "I can feel the heat when I touch Blackfire's hoof. There's that much pressure underneath. One of these times it's going to come pouring out. Then the hoof can start to heal. Until then, there's nothing else we can do."

Dakota mutters something to Hank, then runs upstairs.

Hank plops down on the couch next to me. I've been pretending to watch TV. Now I notice there's nothing on but an infomercial for bald guys.

"You all set for today?" Hank asks. He stares at the TV like I'm doing.

I shrug.

"Hey, sorry about your mom. Dad said it's

166

a setback, but she's going back into the rehab place on Monday, right? So that's good."

I nod. Popeye never told me Mom was going to rehab on Monday. Anger bubbles in my chest. He told Hank and not me. It's not right for Hank to know something about my mother that I don't know.

"Anyway," Hank says, obviously uncomfortable sitting in silence with me and watching a guy get hair planted into his head, "I'll be praying for you and your mom all day."

Hank's for real. I'll give him that. He's not one of those people who always say they'll pray for you but you doubt they ever do. If Hank says he'll pray, I know he will. So now I'm torn between being mad at him for knowing about my mom and being grateful because he's praying for her.

Popeye thunders down the stairs. "Wes, wagons ho! Chicago!"

On the drive to Chicago, Popeye does all the talking. He tells me about Mom going to rehab on Monday. I act like it's news to me.

For the next half hour he tells me about a children's book he's writing. The plot isn't bad—some kid who finds a dog on the roadside, gets attached to him, then meets the owner, who's been searching for the dog. Problem is, Popeye loves rhyme, so he tries to rhyme the whole story. His rhymes are pretty awful. Like, "A dog on the roadside? Now that, I can't abide."

Once we hit heavy traffic, I think we both get a case of nerves. "So," Popeye says, swerving into the slow lane, "what did the little girl say when her dog was lost?"

I shrug, then remember that the last thing I want him to do is look at me for an answer. I don't want him taking his eyes off the road. "I don't know," I answer fast.

"What did the little girl say when her dog was lost? 'Doggone!'"

Neither of us manages much of a laugh.

My mind is on where we're headed. I'm remembering the first time I visited my mother in county lockup. My grandmother made me wear a tie, and I griped and told her Mom wouldn't have made me wear it. I can't remember what the place looked like, but I know my grandma had to talk somebody into letting her go in with me. I sat on her lap behind a glass window. Then my mom walked out and sat in a chair on the other side of the glass. I couldn't touch her or hear her. Grandma talked to her on a phone that gets you through to the person on the other side of the glass. Before we left, Grandma let me talk. I hollered, "I love you!" so loud I wouldn't have needed that phone. We took the bus back, then walked home, and my grandma cried the whole time. That's what I remember most about that day, because my grandma never cried. We'd just gotten to see my mom, and I was feeling good about that. I didn't understand why Grandma cried.

I understand now.

"We're almost there," Popeye says, moving to the exit lane. "Would it be okay if I prayed for you, Wes?"

It's weird that he asked. Popeye prays all the time and never asks if anybody minds. "I don't care," I say.

He doesn't close his eyes, which is a good thing since cars are flying around us. They whiz by and jerk into the slot in front of us.

Popeye starts out thanking God for me and for everybody in his family. Then he gets down to business and prays I'll have the right words to say to my mom, which is the exact thing I've been worrying about. He asks God to take care of Mom and for both of us to find a deep friendship with Jesus.

I try to climb up on that prayer, to have it be from me, too. It feels like I'm holding on to the tail of a comet. I'm hanging on for life.

Popeye finishes his prayer: "Father, will You let Wes know how much You love him and how much You care about his mother? Help them both understand that love and feel Your love, even in jail. I missed the exit!"

Popeye takes the next exit and gets back on the busy expressway in the other direction, then catches the right exit. But it takes too much time getting off and on the highway. He's so slow to jump into the flow of traffic that I want to grab the wheel and stomp the gas pedal. Visiting hour is just that—one hour. We've lost 10 minutes of it already.

By the time we find the right visitors' building, sign in on a clipboard, empty our pockets into a plastic tray, walk through metal detectors, and answer a list of questions about who we are and what we're doing here, we've got less than half of our hour left.

"I'm really sorry, Wes," Popeye says for the 10th time. "I should have left earlier. Then

I missed that exit. I've always been a bad city driver. We should have waited until my Annie could drive us."

Sweat's pooling on his bald head and dripping down the sides of his face. Dark circles are growing like fungus around the armpits of his shirt.

"It's okay, Popeye." I'm not just trying to make him feel better. Since we walked in here, I've stopped rushing. An hour, even a half hour, can be a long time. I don't think I've ever talked to Mom that long.

The waiting room is half-empty, or half-full, depending. It reminds me of a small bus station, with back-to-back chairs in three short rows. A woman is crying in one of the chairs. Behind her, with only the plastic chair backs between them, an older man and woman hold hands and look like they're watching TV, but there's no TV. Three younger women are laughing on the other side of the waiting room while they take off their watches and jewelry and hand them to the guard.

Popeye walks over to the guard and asks, "Could we get in to see the boy's mother now? I got here late, so we're in a hurry."

The laughing women toss me weak smiles full of pity.

I look away. That's when I see the sign: *One visitor at a time.*

"Have a seat over there," the guard says. He doesn't look like a prison guard. He's got white hair, a big belly, and glasses.

Popeye and I take the seats at the end of the crying woman's row because it's closest to the visitation room. A guy comes out of there so fast, the crying woman stops crying. He's got more tattoos than a tattoo parlor. He storms through the waiting room and out the door. The woman goes back to crying.

Finally, the white-haired guard ambles over to us. Popeye and I stand.

"I don't suppose you'd let us go back there together?" Popeye asks.

The guard shakes his head. "One at a time."

"I understand. Can Wes go back, then?" Popeye asks.

"Well, not just yet," the guard answers.

Popeye glances at the wall clock. We're down to 20 minutes left in the visiting hour. "Listen," Popeye pleads, "Wes hasn't seen his mother for months. We're running out of time. Why can't he just go back now?"

The guard points to the sign. "One visitor at a time."

"We know," Popeye says. "I'll wait right here."

"You're not the problem," the guard says. He looks at me. "She's already got a visitor."

"She does?" I can't even imagine who would visit my mother in jail. Or out of jail. She doesn't really have friends she hangs out with, like Dr. Annie does. There aren't any relatives to come visit her. "Who?"

The guard shrugs.

I don't know if he can't tell me or if he won't. "I don't care who it is," I tell him, my chest heaving because it's hard to breathe in this place. "*I'm* the one who's visiting. She knows I'm coming. She's counting on me visiting her."

"Take it easy, son," he says.

But I don't want to take it easy. We're running out of time.

Popeye steps between me and the guard. "Would you please go back and tell his mother that Wes is here?"

"I told her," he says.

My face feels like it's on fire. "Tell her again!" I know he's lying. He's just too lazy to go back there and tell Mom that I'm here.

Popeye puts his hand on my arm, and I realize I've been shouting. The crying woman has stopped crying long enough to stare at me.

"Would you mind, Officer?" Popeye says. "Tell her Wes is out here and really wants to see her."

The guard nods. "I'll tell her." He disappears through the metal door. It closes behind him, leaving Popeye and me standing, waiting.

I have too much time to think. Maybe my mom is mad at me for being late to visit her. Maybe she was so disappointed when I wasn't there that she doesn't want to see me. I should have told the guard to tell her I'm sorry for being late.

I keep checking the clock. Fifteen minutes left. Fourteen. Thirteen. Twelve. "Popeye, why isn't the guard coming back?"

The door swooshes open, and the guard walks out. He goes to the crying woman first, leans down, and says something to her. She stands up fast, picks up her purse, and leaves. Then he strolls toward us.

"I'm sorry," he says.

Thoughts are crashing in my brain like waves on sand, pounding, then backing off, then crashing in another part of my brain until I can't think straight. "What's the matter with her?" I demand. "Is she hurt? Is that why you won't let me see her?"

Popeye puts his hand on my arm, but I shake it off.

"Tell me! Why can't I see my mom?"

The guard takes a deep breath and lets it out. "Son, she says she wants to keep the visitor she's got."

I don't believe him. He's a liar. My mom would never say that. She was counting on me to come and see her. *I* was counting on it.

"Maybe you can come back next time? Work something else out?" the guard suggests. His eyes are soft, sad, filled with pity. I hate looking at him. I hate *him*.

I stare at my shoes. I washed these shoes, my best tennis shoes, even though I knew Mom probably couldn't see my feet. But I washed them just in case.

"Who is it?" I demand. "Who's in there with my mother?"

The guard shakes his head. "I don't know who he is. Why don't you just give it up for today, son." He walks over to the sign-in desk and doesn't look back.

Popeye heads for the receptionist and gets our stuff back, but I stay where I am. When he returns, he says, "Wes, let's go. We'll come back next Saturday if you want to. It will be better in the rehab facility. I'll make sure everything's all set next time. Okay?"

But it's not okay. "I'm not leaving until I see who it is. I want to know who's in there with my mother." A tiny part of me is holding out hope that nobody will walk out, that the guard was lying, that it's all a mix-up, that it's not even my mom back there.

A buzzer sounds the end of visiting hour. People in the waiting room stand. Visitors stream out from the visitation room. A girl who looks about my age is crying. The older couple rush up to her, and they walk out together. I watch two other women, probably wives or girlfriends of prisoners, shuffle down the ramp leading out. One looks dazed, her eyes wide and unfocused. The other looks as natural as if she's just been to the grocery store.

Then I see him. I know instantly that he's the one visiting my mother, even though I haven't seen him in over two years. He hasn't changed. Trolls never change.

He strides down the exit ramp, turns the corner, and stops in front of me. "Mad Dog? Is that you? Man, you getting old, boy! Good to see you. How's the Mad Dog doing these days?"

"Were you in with my mom?" I ask. But it's a stupid question.

He laughs. "On the right side of the bars this time."

Why would she want to talk to him after what he did to her last time? How could she choose him over me?

He stops laughing and sticks out his fat bottom lip. "Hey, man. Your mama feels bad you got yourself up here for nothing. She forgot you was coming."

"What did you say?"

"Huh?" He frowns. "She just forgot you was coming, Mad Dog."

In the last 15 minutes, I've thought of all the reasons, every possible explanation for why my mother didn't let *me* be the one to visit her. Like maybe she had to work out some business thing with this guy. Or maybe she was too scared to kick him out so I could go back and see her. Or maybe she didn't want me to see her in this place.

But never once did I think of this.

She forgot I was coming.

"Well, I gotta bounce, Mad Dog." He's already walking backwards, away from us. "Keep it cool, man." He turns and strolls off.

"Hey," Popeye says, "don't pay any attention to him. Next time, we'll get there an hour early. Annie can drive. We'll get you on the list to see your mom next Saturday."

I shake my head. For months, my mother is all I've thought about. I crossed off days on the calendar. I couldn't sleep because I kept thinking about seeing her today. And she . . . she forgot I was coming.

"No." My voice is calm. Cold.

"Wes?" Popeye sounds worried.

He doesn't need to be. She forgot I was coming. Fine. Now I know where I stand. It makes things simpler. She doesn't need me. And I don't need her.

"I'm not coming back." I can almost feel something inside of me closing. Shutting down. Locking. "I don't ever want to see her again."

SEVENTEEN

POPEYE AND I DON'T TALK ON THE DRIVE HOME. I pretend to be sleeping, but every nerve in my body is wide awake. On alert. My mother forgot. And I'm going to forget too. See how she likes that. She can stay in that jail forever, for all I care.

I don't open my eyes until we pull up at Starlight Animal Rescue and I hear the engine shut off.

Rex is at my door before I can get it open. He jumps on me, begging for his walk. But I don't feel like walking. Or talking. Or thinking. I don't feel like doing anything except going to my room and trying to sleep for real. Forever.

Rex barks. I know him so well that I can tell this isn't a request for a walk. He barks louder, again and again.

Dakota jogs up from the barn. "Didn't go well, huh?" she asks.

I glare at her.

She glances from me to Popeye and back again. "I mean . . . because Rex is barking. I figured Wes must be angry. So it probably didn't go great."

"Stop it, Rex." I head for the house, striding past Kat like I don't see her there with her three cats, all of them mewing for attention. I let the screen door slam behind me before Rex can follow me inside.

"Wes?" Annie pulls off an oven mitt and starts toward me. "I made hamburgers, your favorite. They got a little burned, but I put on extra cheese and onions and—"

"Thanks." I don't look at her. I just keep climbing the stairs that feel even steeper and narrower now. "I'm not hungry." Rex is still barking. I bust into my room and close the door.

Voices from downstairs jumble together. I hear Hank come inside and ask, "What's the matter?" I can't make out the answer.

Then I hear barking, followed by the *click-click* of dog toenails racing up the stairs and down the hall. Rex scratches at my door. He barks and barks.

I have to get to sleep. The dog won't stop barking. My heart pounds as I cross the room and open the door. Rex barks right at me, louder than ever. I take him by the collar and lead him back downstairs and straight out to the porch.

Munch and Bag trot over to welcome Rex, but Rex ignores them. His barking is for nobody but me.

"Sit," I command. Rex sits. "Stay." He stays.

I leave him on the porch and close the door.

The kitchen voices have stopped as suddenly as if I've muted a TV. Without looking at my silent audience, I announce, "Rex is sleeping on the porch with the other dogs." Then I go back to my room, cover my head with my pillow, and hope I never wake up.

☆ ☆ ☆

The next couple of days I do what I have to do, at the Manor and at the Rescue. Dakota helps me walk the dogs. About the only time Rex quits barking around me is when he's on a walk.

I go back to helping Dakota soak Blackfire's hoof. The abscess still hasn't drained, and she gets the vet to come out again. But he says to wait it out. It will come. So we soak the hoof some more.

Dakota and I work all right together as long as we don't talk about anything except the animals. But on Wednesday night when I put Rex out on the porch again, she gets all up in my business. "Wes, I can't take it anymore. What's wrong with you?"

"Nothing's wrong with me," I answer, walking away.

She follows me. "Right. Nothing's wrong with you. That's why you won't talk to us. That's why you're being like this with Rex."

"I'm not doing anything to Rex." I'm half-way up the stairs, but she's right behind me.

"Exactly. You're not doing anything with that poor dog. Rex misses you, Wes. What happened in Chicago? What did your mom say to you that's got you so upset?"

I stop and look at her. "Didn't Popeye tell

you?" I figured he would have told the whole family how my mother stood me up at the jail.

Dakota shakes her head. "He said it was your business and you'd talk about it when you wanted to."

"He's right." But I'm still surprised he didn't tell her.

"You can't keep everything inside," Dakota pleads. "Anybody with eyes can see it's eating you alive. You keep everything inside like that, and . . . and it'll fester, just like Blackfire's hoof."

I don't want to hear this. It cuts too close to home. When I touch the horse's hoof where the sore is in deep, too deep to see, I can feel the heat from inside. I picture the pus and junk growing in there. And that's what it feels like inside of me when I think about my mother.

"Just leave me alone, Dakota."

✷ ✷ ✷

On Thursday, Ms. Bean calls to tell me that my mother is out of jail. She's back in rehab, and I can visit her there on Saturday if I want to.

Thanks, but no thanks.

Everybody leaves me alone until Friday, when we're scheduled to take the dogs to Nice Manor for another training session. That morning, it's like the dogs have gotten together to plot how to make it hardest on Mad Dog. Moxie gets so scared that she wets the rug inside the door the second she gets back from her walk. Munch has a wild outbreak of the slobbers. Bag won't leave me alone because he wants to play. Rex barks the whole time. And I can't find the three-legged Lion. I have to search the house and the yard before I find the Pom curled up with Kat in her bed.

"Mrs. Coolidge is here!" Dakota yells.

The horn honks that stupid *Duh duh-duh-duh duh! Duh!* tune.

I snatch the Pom without waking Kat and head to the car.

Mrs. Coolidge revs the engine when I walk out, just in case I didn't get that the horn honking meant she was in a hurry and I was making her late.

When we're all in and strapped, she takes off. "So, what do you really think about that activities director?" Mrs. Coolidge asks.

"She's okay," Dakota answers when I

don't. "I thought she was creepy when we first met her, but she's been joining in on the training sessions. She's helping me with Munch, and she's not the brightest bulb in the pack."

"Carol's a good kid. We were in the same class at Nice High, although we didn't have much in common. She had a big crush on Mr. Coolidge Senior, God rest his soul. Sometimes I wonder if she's gotten over him yet." She's quiet for a minute. Then she almost whispers, "The man made it hard for a body to get over him."

Dakota tries to get her to tell more, but Mrs. Coolidge refuses to go there.

At Nice Manor, everybody knows what to do by now. They sit in pairs and buddy up on dogs. I've told Dakota that this is a review day for voice commands, so she goes over the instructions with the group.

"Make sure your leashes are on," she shouts over the barking from Munch and Bag. "One person should hold the dog, and your partner should stand three feet away, holding the end of the leash. Tell your dog to come. Then gently tug the leash to make sure he obeys."

I walk around the room and observe. We've done this before, but they still don't get it. "Don't forget," I remind Rose and Velva. "Call your dog by his name. Not Baby Doll or Sweetie Pie or my Precious."

Leon and Buddy are laughing and joking around. Buddy calls Munch like a catcher would taunt a guy up to bat. "Come on, Munchster! You can do it, girl!"

"Aren't you guys listening?" I ask. "Use the dog's name–her *real* name–first. Then 'come.' Is that so hard? 'Munch, come.'"

When Munch doesn't come, I take the leash and tug. Maybe I tug a little too hard, but the dog comes.

Dakota pipes up. "Remember that asking a dog to come is an invitation. You don't want to use it as a punishment, or they'll never want to come to you. And *never* train a dog when you're angry." She acts like she's instructing all of us. But I know her words are for me.

And I don't appreciate it. "Fine!" I snap. "*You* take it from here." I get out of the room as fast as I can. I don't need this. Why should I go to all this trouble anyway? It's not my problem.

I hear the squeaking wheels of a wheelchair come up behind me.

Buddy rolls around so I have to face her. "What was all that about, Wes?"

"Nothing."

She peers at me. "I knew a third baseman once who carried around so much anger and bitterness with him, the slightest thing set him off. Got thrown out of more games than most people play in a lifetime."

There's nothing to say to that, except "Who cares?" And I won't say that to her.

"What happened last weekend when you saw your mama?" Buddy asks.

"Nothing," I snap.

"How's that?" she asks.

Finally, I return her stare. "Nothing happened because I didn't see her. Okay? She forgot I was coming. When she found out I was there waiting, it didn't matter to her. She didn't want to see me. There. Satisfied?"

Buddy doesn't look away. She doesn't blink. "I can see why you're so bitter, Wes."

Bitter. I hadn't put it into a word, but that one fits. Like a bad taste in my mouth, a sourness that won't go away, that keeps forcing its way up like vomit. I'm bitter all right. "So what if I am?" My throat burns with the words.

"Wouldn't *you* be bitter if your mother did that to *you*?"

"Likely I would, and that's the truth," she admits. She pats her legs. "My mama gave me these legs. She was a drinker. I was four years old when she piled me into the car one night and headed for the liquor store. When she plowed into an 18-wheeler, people said it was a miracle she didn't kill us both. She broke her thumb. It healed. My legs didn't."

In my head, I see the whole thing. The truck coming at them. The crash. The hospital. "What did you do?"

"Carried around a whole mess of bitterness most of my life. Till I met up with a left fielder who told me, 'Buddy, bitterness is like swallowing poison and expecting the other guy to get sick and die.'"

. . . like swallowing poison and expecting the other guy to get sick . . .

I start to ask her to say it again, to tell me more about her mother. But before I can get out a single word, the door to the rec room opens, and Miss Golf walks out.

"There you are." She shuffles up to me, her back to Buddy. "Wes, I wanted to tell you the good news. I met with the directors of Nice Manor. We talked to the state board. They've okayed the dog program."

Buddy whistles through her teeth. "Go, team!" she shouts.

Miss Golf smiles, showing a row of white overbite. "Plus, they said we could take two dogs. Two! Isn't that grand? I just couldn't believe–!"

"Two?" I ask. I glance through the window and see Dakota working with Moxie. Leon is on the floor, rolling around with Munch. Bag is playing fetch with June. I don't see Lion, but I know he's there. "What about the others?"

Miss Golf's smile fades. "Well, I'm not sure. But, Wes, I wasn't even sure the board would okay one dog, much less two."

"But we have *four* dogs!" I insist. "Four!"

Her eyes are getting big, and I know I'm too loud. But I can't help it. "Four dogs who need homes and people to love them. Four dogs, and all they want is someone to care about them. Someone who'll care enough about them to think about them. Maybe even to love them. Is that too much to ask?"

I turn my back on Nice Manor and run

outside. I'm done with this. From now on, Buddy and Miss Golf and Mrs. Coolidge and everybody else can do whatever they want. And they can do it without the help of Mad Dog Williams.

EIGHTEEN

THE MINUTE WE DRIVE UP THE LANE to Starlight Animal Rescue, Rex is there. He never chases cars, but he's chasing us now. His bark sets off a chain reaction of barking dogs inside the car.

I jump out as soon as the car pulls to a stop. "Rex, no!" I shout. "Bad dog!"

Hank steps out from the barn and hollers for Dakota. "I need help with your horse, Dakota! Hurry up!"

She runs off, leaving me to lug the kennels by myself. Fine. I don't need her. I lift Munch's kennel out, then Bag's. They're barking because Rex still won't lay off. I've got Lion in one arm, so I try to coax Moxie out of the backseat. But she won't come.

"Be quiet, Rex!" I shout. This makes Moxie retreat farther into the back of the car.

"I'm late for my bridge game," Mrs. Coolidge says. She has both hands on the steering wheel.

Popeye jogs up. I think he must have come from the house, but I didn't see it. I can't see or hear anything except Rex and his earsplitting barks. Popeye climbs into the backseat and comes out with Moxie. "There you go, little gal."

Mrs. Coolidge waves, then takes off.

Rex doesn't chase after the car like a normal dog would. I want him to. I want him to get away from me and quit barking. I bend down and pick up a stick. "Rex! Go!" I toss the stick clear across the yard.

For a second, the barking stops. Rex takes off after the stick. In a flash, he's back. He drops the stick at my feet and starts barking again.

Popeye says something, but I can't hear him. I can't hear anything except the barking. It's louder and louder. Or maybe it's just in my head, growing. Like bitterness. Like an abscess. Bigger and louder. Until I can't stand it anymore.

"Stop it!" I cry.

Rex barks even louder, if that's possible. He won't stop.

"He's just warning you about your anger, Wes," Popeye says.

I don't need a dog to tell me how angry I am. "Go! Don't you get it, you stupid dog? I don't want you here! I don't want *you*!" I kick the dirt. My shoe catches the stick. It flips into the air.

Rex whimpers and dodges the stick. It bangs to the ground. I pick it up and throw it, hard, as far as I can. "Go! Go away! I don't want you anymore!"

Rex turns to me, his brown eyes big and unblinking. His head drops and he trots off, tail between his legs.

My legs crumple under me. I collapse to the ground. My whole body is shaking. I can't control it. My heart's pounding in my chest so hard I can barely breathe. And then tears burst out of me, all at once, like a volcano erupting from deep inside.

"It's okay, Wes." Popeye is sitting on the

ground next to me. He's close, but he doesn't touch me. I think I'd scream if he touched me. My skin is too hot.

"Father, comfort Wes," Popeye whispers. "Let him feel how much You love him."

I don't know how long we sit there, with me shaking and Popeye muttering words that have to be prayers.

Finally, when I think I can talk, I say, "I didn't mean it. I didn't want Rex to go."

"I know," Popeye says. "Rex knows."

The air is still. Waiting.

"How could she forget?"

A minute passes, time enough for me to relive everything. I'm mad at Mom for signing herself out of rehab. I'm mad that she started using again, that she went back to the guy we both swore we'd never let into our lives again, that she didn't kick him out of the visiting room when she heard I was there to see her.

But what gets me more than anything is that I wasn't even a part of her thoughts. She forgot about me.

I turn to Popeye. "How can she not even think about me?"

"You don't know that, Wes," Popeye answers.

"What would you know about it?" I snap. "You don't know how it feels not having anybody give you a single thought. Ever."

"Wes, God thinks about you *all* the time."

"Yeah, right." Maybe God thinks about Popeye. Popeye's the kind of person God would like thinking about. Not me. My own mother doesn't even like thinking about me.

"'How precious are your thoughts about me, O God. They cannot be numbered! I can't even count them; they outnumber the grains of sand! And when I wake up, you are still with me!' That's from Psalm 139," Popeye explains.

God's thoughts outnumber the grains of sand. God's thoughts about me?

I want to drink in the words. I want to believe that God thinks about *me* like that. More thoughts than I can count. Imagining this feels like water running over me. I close my eyes and try to picture God thinking about me. But I can't picture God. So I picture Jesus. And it's easier to think about the Jesus who hung out with losers, the Jesus who healed people and died for them—*that* Jesus. I can almost imagine Him caring, thinking about me.

"Father," Popeye prays, "help Wes know, understand, and believe how much You love him. Help him accept that love and forgiveness through Christ."

I grab on to the comet of Popeye's prayer. Only it doesn't feel like I'm borrowing his words this time. It feels like I'm praying them for myself. *Thank You.* I'm not sure if I say the words out loud. But I know God hears me. I sense that He's listening . . . and thinking about me.

"And thanks for thinking about Wes's mother, too," Popeye says. "And for loving her like—"

"Wait." I open my eyes. I don't want to go where he's going. I'm not ready. I want him to keep my mother out of this.

Popeye looks up. Then he smiles, but not at me. He's grinning at something behind me.

I turn around, and I'm pounced on by Rex. I let myself fall backwards in the grass. My dog puts one paw on my chest, then drops the stick from his mouth and licks my face. I cover my head, but Rex is determined. He licks and licks.

I throw my arms around his neck. "I'm so sorry, Rex. Good Rex. I love you, boy." He lets me hug him while he lunges at me, scoring more licks on my face. His tail wags so hard it slaps my knees.

"Forgive me, boy?" I beg.

"What do you think?" Popeye says. He pets my dog. "That dog has already forgiven you. He loves you no matter what. He'll keep on loving you no matter what. Unconditionally."

I know Popeye's right. Rex always loves me, even when I ignore him or yell at him. And I know Popeye's not just talking about Rex. "You're trying to tell me that's how God loves me, right?"

Popeye laughs. "That's just a taste of how God loves you, Wes. Now multiply that by more numbers than you can count, and you're still not there."

I nod. But in my heart I'm shouting.

I bury my face in Rex's neck and remember my mom the way I saw her last. Her eyes were bloodshot. Her whole body looked broken.

She needs to know she's not alone. She needs to know Somebody's thinking about her too.

I sit up, but I keep holding my dog. "Popeye?" I ask. I have the sensation that I'm being watched. Thought about. Loved.

"What, Wes?" Popeye says.

"Do you think we could still go see my mom tomorrow?"

NINETEEN

"WES, WAIT!" Dakota races from the barn at full speed.

Popeye, Annie, and I are in the minivan, ready to drive to Chicago. I'm taking Lion with me. I want my mom to meet our new dog.

Miss Golf from Nice Manor called late last night to tell us that Moxie and Bag could move into the Manor whenever they're ready. She's taking Munch home with her as her own dog. It was like everything worked out the way it was supposed to, with me keeping the Pom for Mom and me, whenever Mom's better. Even before I hung up the phone, I was thanking

God for knowing all along that things would work out.

Dakota runs to the van and comes right up to the open window on my side. "It worked! The abscess broke. All the gunk is out of the hoof. Hank says Blackfire should heal fast now."

"That's great, Dakota." I know what that feels like. Inside of me, the gunk is draining out too. I'm healing.

"Gotta go!" Popeye shouts.

Dakota moves in closer and whispers, "Are you sure about this? What if your mother . . . ? I mean, what if . . . ?"

"It'll be okay, Dakota," I tell her.

Annie drives and makes better time than Popeye did. He tells dog jokes most of the way there. But this time I can tell he's not doing it to keep my mind off the visit. He's just being Popeye. Lion and I ride in the backseat and watch the scenery.

The rehab place isn't much better than county lockup. We have to leave our valuables and empty our pockets. We knew there was a good chance they wouldn't let the dog in, and it turns out "no pets" is one of the million rules that go with rehab.

"Popeye and I can wait outside with Lion," Annie says. "You go on ahead. Don't worry about us. Take all the time you need."

I find my mom on a faded green couch in a dingy living room. The room's not much bigger than what we had above the bar, and we're not the only ones in it. A woman and a girl, probably her daughter, are arguing in whispers by the window. Another woman, who looks older than Mom, sits in a rocking chair and flips magazine pages faster than anybody could read.

I sit next to Mom and kiss her cheek. She lifts her shoulders and doesn't turn away. We exchange small talk, like we're strangers who saw each other only yesterday.

After a few minutes, I run out of things to say. So I blurt out, "I brought you a dog, but they wouldn't let him in. He's only got three legs, but he's cute. You'll like him."

"Wesley Williams!" she says, coming to life. "A dog? What on earth would I do with a dog? I don't need no dog."

I feel the anger creep into the corners of my head, but I don't let it in. Instead, I think about Jesus thinking about me and thinking about Mom, and even Lion.

"That's okay, Mom," I tell her.

She shakes her head. Then she puts her hand on mine. "Wes, Wes, what were you thinking?"

I grin at her. I don't know why, but it's okay. What *am* I thinking? I'm thinking about thinking. In all the thoughts God has about me, I'm pretty sure He's got this all worked out. He's not surprised that my mom doesn't like dogs. Maybe He'll work on her.

We have another awkward silence. Panic seeps in because I can't think of anything to say to my mother. So I shoot up a quick prayer and ask God what He'd say, and I go with that.

✳ ✳ ✳

Back outside, I find Popeye and Annie playing with Lion in a tiny, dried-up garden.

Popeye sees me first. "Hey, Wes! Watch this." He turns to Lion. "Lion, why do dogs wag their tails?" Lion wags his tail. "Why do dogs wag their tails? Because nobody else will wag it for them."

The whole drive home, I tell Annie and Popeye about my visit with Mom. When we drive up at Starlight Animal Rescue, everybody's waiting for us. Dakota and Hank are tossing a football. Kat is sitting on a blanket with her cats surrounding her. Even old Mrs. Coolidge is there, sitting on a lawn chair with Rex at her feet.

Dakota jogs to the car and takes Lion from me. Rex comes bounding over. I get out of the car and hug my dog. His breath smells like cold hot dogs.

"So?" Dakota asks. "How did your mom like Lion? Is she excited about having a three-legged Pomeranian for her very own?"

I shake my head. "Nope. She doesn't like dogs, even three-legged Poms."

"But . . ." Dakota fumbles for the words. "I thought . . . I mean . . . Wes, what gives? Your mom told you she doesn't want the dog?"

"Yeah." The sun is setting behind the barn, swallowing Starlight Animal Rescue in a bank of purple clouds.

"So?" Dakota demands. She points to my dog. "I don't get it."

Rex is curled up at my feet, his head against my leg.

"What do you mean?" But then I get it.

I reach down and pet my dog. He lifts his head and pants. With his tongue hanging out, it looks like he's laughing.

I laugh too. If I needed proof that God is for real, that He's thinking about me and changing me, well, here it is. "You're right, Rex."

Hank calls over from the grill. "What are you laughing at, Wes?"

Kat moves in closer, her favorite cat wrapped around her neck like a shawl. "Yeah. And what is Rex right about?"

Rex paws my leg, asking me to pet him. I put my hand on his head. "Rex is right about me, Kat. He's not barking."

Tips on Finding the Perfect Pet

- Talk with your whole family about owning a pet. Pets require a commitment from every member of the family. Your pet should be around for years—ten, fifteen, twenty, twenty-five, or thirty years, depending on the type of pet. Pets can be expensive, especially if they get sick or need medical care of any kind. Make sure you can afford to give your pet a good life for a long time.

- Think like your future pet. Would you be happy with the lifestyle in your house? Would you spend most of your time alone? Is there room for you in the house? If you're considering buying a horse, what kind of life will the horse have? Will someone be able to spend enough time caring for it?

- Study breeds and characteristics of the animal you're considering. Be prepared to spend time with your pet, bonding and training, caring and loving.

- Remember that there is no such thing as a perfect pet, just as there's no such thing as a perfect owner. Both you and your pet will need to work to develop the best possible relationship you can have and to become lifelong best friends.

Consider Pet Adoption

- Check out animal rescue organizations, such as the humane society (www.hsus .org), local shelters, SPCA (www.spca.com), 1-800-Save-A-Pet.com (PO Box 7, Redondo Beach, CA 90277), Pets911.com (great horse adoption tips), and Petfinder.com. Adopting a pet from a shelter will save that pet's life and make room for another animal, who might also find a good home.

- Take your time. Visit the shelters and talk with the animal caregivers. Legitimate shelters will be able to provide you with documentation on the animal's health and medical records. Find out all you can. Ask questions. Who owned the pet before? How many owners were there? Why was the pet given away? Is the pet housebroken? Does it like children?

- Consider adopting an adult pet. People tend to favor the "babies," but adopting a fully grown animal may be less risky. What you see is what you get. The personality and size and manners are there for you to consider.

Rescuing Animals

- It's great that you want to help every animal you meet. I wish everyone felt the same. But remember that safety has to come first. A frightened, abused animal can strike out at any time. If you find an animal that's in trouble, call your local animal shelter. Then try to find the owner.

- The best way to help a lost pet find its home again is to ask around. Ask friends, neighbors, classmates, the newspaper deliverer, and the mail carrier. You might put a "Found Pet" ad in the paper or make flyers with the animal's picture on it. But be sure to report the find to your local shelter because that's where most owners will go for help in finding a lost pet.

- Report animal cruelty to your local animal shelter, to the humane society, or to organizations like Pets911 (www.pets911.com/services/animalcruelty).

AUTHOR TALK

DANDI DALEY MACKALL grew up riding horses, taking her first solo bareback ride when she was three. Her best friends were Sugar, a Pinto; Misty, probably a Morgan; and Towaco, an Appaloosa. Dandi and her husband, Joe; daughters, Jen and Katy; and son, Dan, (when forced) enjoy riding Cheyenne, their Paint. Dandi has written books for all ages, including Little Blessings books, *Degrees of Guilt: Kyra's Story, Degrees of Betrayal: Sierra's Story, Love Rules, Maggie's Story,* and the best-selling series Winnie the Horse Gentler. Her books (about 450 titles) have sold more than 4 million copies. She writes and rides from rural Ohio.

Visit Dandi's Web site at
www.dandibooks.com

Winnie The Horse Gentler

Can't get enough of Winnie? Visit her Web site to read more about Winnie and her friends plus all about their horses.

IT'S ALL ON WINNIETHEHORSEGENTLER.COM
There are so many fun and cool things to do on Winnie's Web site; here are just a few:

★ PAT'S PETS
Post your favorite photo of your pet and tell us a fun story about them

★ ASK WINNIE
Here's your chance to ask Winnie questions about your horse

★ MANE ATTRACTION
Meet Dandi and her horse, Cheyenne!

★ THE BARNYARD
Here's your chance to share your thoughts with others

★ AND MUCH MORE!